To Luci,

Happy 19th Birthday,

all my love,
Rebecca
xox


A study of a mother
and daughter- for Luci.

*The Time:*
*Night*

# *The Time: Night*

**LUDMILLA PETRUSHEVSKAYA**

*Translated from the Russian by*
SALLY LAIRD

Published by VIRAGO PRESS Limited 1994
20–23 Mandela Street, Camden Town,
London NW1 0HQ

First published in Russian in *Novy Mir*, No. 2, 1992

The translator would like to thank Natalia Perova for her
kind help in reviewing the first draft of this translation.

*A CIP catalogue record for this title is available
from the British Library*

Typeset by Florencetype Ltd, Kewstoke, Avon
Printed in Great Britain by Mackays of Chatham plc

*The phone rang, and a woman's voice said:*
*'Sorry to bother you, but after Mum . . .' There was a*
*pause. 'When Mum died she left some manuscripts. I*
*thought maybe you'd like to have a look at them. She was*
*a poet. I know you're very busy . . . Of course, if you*
*haven't the time. Of course. Sorry to bother you.'*
*Two weeks later the manuscripts came in the post, a*
*dusty file stuffed with loose pages, children's exercise*
*books, blank telegram forms all covered in writing. The*
*whole thing was subtitled 'Notes from the edge of the*
*table'. There was no name given, no return address.*

# The Time:
# Night

He can't understand that when you're out visiting you don't just rush up to people's dressing-tables and start grabbing things all the little vases and knick-knacks and scent bottles, and especially the little jewellery cases. And you don't ask straight out for seconds. He's a child of hungry times, my Tima – whenever I take him to someone's house he starts rootling around, meddling with everything, discovers a toy car under the bed and decides on the spot it's his and is thrilled to bits, clasps the thing to his breast and rushes up beaming to say Look what I've found! Under the bed! And of course it was my friend Masha had given the toy to her little grandson, a nice American car, it'd rolled under the bed and he'd forgotten all about it, but out comes Masha all anxious from the kitchen and there's her little Denis and my Tima at each other's throats. They've got a nice postwar apartment, we'd come to beg a loan off them to see us through till the pension came in; they'd just polished off dinner when we arrived, came out of the kitchen licking their greasy lips and Masha had had to go right back in there to see if there was anything in the larder they could bear to spare us. So anyway there was little Denis trying to grab his car back while my Tima was clutching the wretched thing with all his might and main, and of course Denis has a whole car showroom, rows and rows of them – he's nine years old and a strapping great lad. So I tore Tima away from Denis and his car, Tima was mad at me but what could I do, that would be the last we'd see of them – as it was, Masha had thought twice before opening the door when she'd seen us through the peephole! It all wound up with me taking him off to the bathroom to wash his tear-stained face – fancy throwing a tantrum in someone else's house! That's why people don't want to see us, because of Tima. Of course I behave like the Queen of England, say no thanks to everything, won't touch a thing – not even the sugar and crackers to go with my tea. I'll only drink their tea with the bread I've brought, keep tearing off little mouthfuls to stay the pangs, it's unbearable to sit starving at someone else's table! But Tima sets right to work on the crackers and then starts asking can't he have a bit of butter (the butter's still sitting

2

there on the table). 'What about you?' asks Masha, but the only thing I care about is feeding Tima, so no thanks, spread a bit more on for Tima – Tima darling would you like a bit more? I see Denis giving us sidelong glances from the doorway, not to mention the son-in-law Vladimir who's gone off to have a smoke on the stairs outside and his wife Oksana who comes straight into the kitchen knowing very well all my troubles, and right in front of Tima – she looks a picture of health herself – she says:

'So, Auntie Anya' – that's me – 'Do you see anything of Alyona these days? Does your mummy ever come and see you, Tima?'

'Dunechka dear,' I say – that's Oksana's nickname from when she was little – 'surely I told you? Alyona's not well, she's got terrible mastitis.'

'Mastitis???' (meaning where on earth has she gone and got mastitis, what's she doing feeding a baby?)

I quickly grab a few more crackers, nice creamy ones, and hurry Tima out of the kitchen to watch television in the living-room – off we go now, *Good Night* is going to be on in a minute (actually there's still half an hour to go).

And she follows us in there saying what if it got round at Alyona's work that she'd left her own child to the mercy of fate? Very interesting, is that what I'm supposed to be? The mercy of fate?

'What work, Oksana dear? How can she go to work if she's feeding a baby!'

So finally she asks who was it then, not the one Alyona used to go on about on the phone – about how she never knew it could be like this, it was out

3

of this world, she kept crying, waking up and crying from happiness? That one, was it? The one she had when she kept asking us to lend her the money to buy an apartment, but we couldn't have, we were try-ing to get a new car at the time and repair the dacha? It was him, was it? Or who then? I tell her I've no idea.

And the point of this interrogation, of course, was to make quite sure we'd never come and see them again. Though once upon a time they'd been friends, she and Alyona, years back when they were little – we had a holiday together once on the Baltic, there was I with my husband and children, all young and suntanned, and there was Masha with her little Dunechka; Masha at the time was recovering from a wretched affair, she'd chased after a man and fetched up having an abortion; he wouldn't give up his family, wouldn't give up anything – his little model Tomik and Tusya from Leningrad, Masha knew all about them but I'd fanned the flames inadvertently because I knew yet another woman of his at the Film Institute, she was famous for her huge thighs and for what happened after she got married: she'd got a summons in the post from the VD clinic, saying she'd missed one of her regular injections for gonorrhoea, and he'd just gone and dumped her, said goodbye from the window of his Volga, and when she'd run weeping after the car – she was still just a student then – he'd thrown an envelope out through the window, and in it – she'd stopped to pick it up – were some dollars, but not very many. He was a professor of some sort, a Lenin expert. So anyway there was Masha left with

4

her Dunechka up on the Baltic and me and my husband trying to entertain her; she'd follow us wearily down to the local dive at Maiori, all hung with nets inside it was I remember, and we always ended up paying for her, you only live once after all and who cares, though she was the one with the sapphire earrings and all. She looked at my plastic bracelet – a simple little modern thing, Czech-made, cost me a rouble twenty – she looked at it once and said: 'Is that a serviette ring?' 'Yes,' said I, and put it on my wrist.

But time went by, and I don't just mean my getting the sack, but the fact is Masha and I always were and always will be poles apart in terms of living standards. Anyway, there was her son-in-law Vladimir sitting watching the telly – that's the reason they're always so quarrelsome in the evening, any moment now Denis, as usual, was going to start fighting his dad to have *Good Night* on, and my Tima only gets to see it once in a blue moon so he starts on at Vladimir too: 'Oh please! Oh go on, please!' – holds his hands up in prayer, virtually sinks to his knees – just imitating me, alas. Alas.

Vladimir's got something against Tima and he's sick to death of Denis; in fact it's obvious, between you and me, that he's on the way out, Oksana's husband, he's on the wane – that's why Oksana's so poisonous these days. He's writing his thesis on Lenin too, they can't get off the subject in that family, though Masha publishes all sorts of things, she's an editor in a publishing house, they specialise in calendars, in fact Masha used to wangle me the odd commission for them now and then, very hoity-toity

5

she always was about it too – though in fact it was me saved her skin that time, I dashed off an article about the two hundredth anniversary of a tractor factory in Minsk but the fee she gave me was even mingier than I'd expected; unbeknownst to me it turned out I was just the 'co-author', the other author was the chief engineer at the factory – they always do it like that, makes it look more authoritative. And how I suffered for it – afterwards she said I wasn't to show my face there for at least five years, apparently someone had written in to ask how on earth a tractor factory could be celebrating its two hundredth anniversary – had the first Russian tractor been launched or rolled off the conveyor belt, whatever, in seventeen hundred and something?

So as I say there's Vladimir the son-in-law sitting watching the telly, ears all aflame so it must have been some important match, and then it's the same old story! Denis sits down on the floor and starts bawling, Tima rushes to the rescue but, clumsy kid, pokes his finger blindly at the telly, whereupon the wretched thing goes off altogether, the son-in-law jumps up with a howl of rage, I'm standing there at the ready but Vladimir hauls himself off to the kitchen to fetch his wife and mother-in-law – thank God at least he recollected himself in time and didn't lay hands on my poor orphan himself. Meanwhile Denis had pushed the flustered Tima away, turned the thing back on and was sitting peacefully watching his cartoon, and Tima had joined in and was chuckling away with great gusto.

But nothing ever turns out that simple – Vladimir had gone and read the riot act to the women, told his sob story from beginning to end, demanding blood and threatening to leave (at least that's what I guess was going on), so Masha comes in looking all sorrowful like someone who's done a good deed and look at the thanks she gets. And after her comes Vladimir with a face like a gorilla. He's got a handsome face, not unlike Charles Darwin – though not at that particular moment; at that particular moment he looked thoroughly low-down, brutish and mean.

In short it was the usual scenario – the two women started yelling at Denis, and Tima by this time was past caring, he'd had it up to here with all their shrieking – just made his funny little grimace, it's his nervous tic. Of course by yelling at Denis they were really yelling at us. My poor little orphan, poor little orphan . . . the eternal refrain of our life these days . . .

We had an even better time at someone else's house – Tima and I had dropped in on some distant acquaintances, we couldn't ring first because they didn't have a phone, so we just arrived, went in, and there they were sitting at table. Tima: 'Grandma, I'm hungry too!' Oh dear, we've had such a long walk, the child's got hungry, let's go home, Tima darling, I'd only wanted to ask whether you might have had word of Alyona (it was an ex-colleague of hers' family, they kept in touch now and then). So the ex-colleague gets up from the table and slowly, like in a dream, ladles out a bowlful each of rich meaty borsch – oh goodnessme, we really hadn't expected . . .

'We haven't heard a thing from Alyona.'

7

Is the girl alive?

'She hasn't been round, we don't have a phone at home and she never phones at work, anyway at work you're always here there and everywhere, either it's the membership dues have to be collected or it's something else . . . bread?'

'You really shouldn't . . . how kind . . . We won't stay for the main course, thank you very much, I can see you're tired, you've come straight from work. Well maybe just a bit for little Tima. Tima dear, would you like some meat? Just a bit for him, then, just a bit' (suddenly I burst into tears, it's a weakness of mine). And then all of a sudden a nasty Alsatian bitch comes shooting out from under the bed and bites Tima on the elbow. Tima starts shrieking with his mouth full of meat, and the father of the household – he looks vaguely like Charles Darwin too – hauls himself from the table and starts shouting and threatening – supposedly addressing the wretched dog of course. So that's that, that's the last time we can show our faces here, I'd kept this house in reserve for use *in extremis*. But that's it now, *in extremis* I'll have to find some other way out.

Oh Alyona, my distant daughter. Love is the most important thing in life, I do believe it. What have I done to deserve all this? I loved her to distraction! Loved my Andrei to distraction! Infinitely, infinitely, loved them both!

Anyway it's all over now, my life's done with, though

no one would believe it to look at me – just the other day someone mistook me for a young girl from behind: Excuse me, young lady – oh! I beg your pardon, madam, do you know the way to such and such street? He was all dirty and sweaty but not short of money, by the look of it, and he looked at me so sweetly – all the hotels are full up, he says, that's the problem. Oh, we know your type! Oh yes! For half a kilo of pomegranates he wants a free night's lodging, not to mention a few other little services – so it's make up the bed and put the kettle on, fasten the hook on my door so he can't come begging – I took the whole thing in at first glance. Like a chess player. I'm a poet. Some people like the word 'poetess', but look what Tsvetaeva said – or Akhmatova – my almost name-sake, we have this mystic link between us, there's only a few letters' difference: she's Anna Andreevna and I'm Anna too, but Andrianovna in my case. Whenever I get to give a reading I always ask them to announce me as 'the poet Anna . . .' (with my husband's surname). The way they listen to me, those children! I know the way to a child's heart. And Tima comes everywhere with me, I go up on the stage and Tima comes and sits right there at the table with me, he'll never go and sit with the audience. He sits there and puckers his lips, poor fellow, it's his nervous tic. So I stroke his hair and make my little joke: 'Tamara and I go everywhere together' – and invariably some idiot, one of the organisers, starts shouting 'Why doesn't little Tamara come and sit in the audience' – they don't realise I'm just quoting a bit of verse.

Of course Tima then pipes up: I'm not Tamara, he says, getting all in a huff, and then he won't even say thank you for the sweets, just obstinately climbs up on the stage and sits down beside me at the table. Very soon, Tima darling, no one's going to invite me anywhere to read, d'you realise? – and all because of you. He's so withdrawn poor child it makes you weep, of course he's had such a difficult time. He's so quiet and still sometimes, my little shining star. He does shine, that boy of mine, he always smells of flowers. When he was tiny and I used to empty his potty I always noticed how it smelled like camomile, his pee, and his hair when it hasn't been washed for a while smells just like phlox. And when he's been washed all over the smell of him's inexpressible, that lovely fresh scent of a child's body. His silky little toes, his silky hair. What could be lovelier than a child! That silly fool Galina at the place I used to work once said to me: If only you could make a handbag (silly fool!) out of a child's cheeks – she went into raptures at the thought, ridiculous woman, dreaming of a child's-skin handbag, though of course she was mad about her own little boy; she once said to me – ages ago now – she told me once what a lovely little bottom he had, couldn't take her eyes off it. That's all over now, of course; that little bottom of hers is doing his duty in the army these days.

How quickly it all fades! You feel so helpless looking in the mirror, still the same person and yet there you are, all gone . . . come on Grandma let's go says

10

Tima the moment we've got to the reading; he can't bear it, he's jealous of my success, wants everyone to know I'm his grandma. But what can I do, sweetheart, your Anna has to earn a crust for herself (I call myself Anna to him). And for you too, demanding little wretch, not to mention Granny Sima, thank God Alyona at least gets her alimony, but of course Andrei needs the extra because of his foot (of which more anon); he's been completely crippled by prison life. That's the thing . . . So one reading earns me eleven roubles, sometimes just seven, and if I get a couple of them a month it's thanks to Nadya, that angel, I sink to my knees in gratitude before her. Once Andrei went to see her, I'd asked him to take round some documents she needed, and can you imagine he went and begged ten roubles off her when she hadn't a bean! Poor Nadya with her legless invalid mother! Oh how I cringed, the contortions I went through . . . You don't need to tell me, I whispered to her – there was a whole crowd of us there, all poets-for-life like me – you don't need to tell me, I know how it is, my old mother's been in hospital heaven knows how long . . .

How long is it now? Seven years. It's a torture going there every week, she gobbles up everything I bring right there in front of me, goes into floods and complains how her fellow-patients eat up all her food when in fact, as the matron told me, none of the old ladies can get out of their beds, so what's she complaining about? You'd do better not to come, matron said, it just sets the cat among the patients was how she put it. She said the same thing just recently after Tima had been ill and I hadn't been

11

there a month. I'm telling you firmly, don't come. Firmly, she said.

And Andrei turns up regularly to claim his share. Why on earth, I can't help asking, he's got a wife, why not make do with her. What does he want from me? Why, I ask you, why suck your mother dry and steal from Granny Sima and the kid? Why, why, why, he answers, just let me rent out my room for seventy roubles, then I won't need anything from you. What room? I ask in amazement for the nth time, all of us are registered here: Granny Sima, me, Alyona and her two children and only then you, you come last, and anyway you're living at your wife's. Five square metres is all you're entitled to here. So there and then he starts calculating out loud: if a fifteen-square-metre room costs seventy roubles – God knows why he keeps insisting like an idiot on this seventy roubles – then seventy divided by three is twenty-three roubles thirty-three kopecks. Well okay, he concedes, you pay twenty roubles for the apartment, why don't you divide it in six and rent it out? Then you'll owe me exactly twenty roubles a month. All right then, Andrei, I say, in that case I'll put in a claim for maintenance from you, okay? In that case, says he, I'll inform them that you're already getting the alimony from Tima's dad. Miserable creature! He doesn't realise that I don't get a bean, and if he ever found out, if he ever found out . . . He'd be round at Alyona's work like a shot putting in his claim for heaven knows how much. Alyona knows the score and keeps right out of harm's way, right out of harm's way, and of course I'm not going to tell on her. She rents a place somewhere for herself and the kid, can't imagine how she pays for it. If you work it out: the alimony comes to fifty roubles, then there's her single mother's benefit and the extra nursing mother's allowance she gets from work for the first year, and that's it. God only knows how she makes out. Maybe the baby's father pays for the apartment? Of course she never lets on who she's living with or whether she's got a man at all; all she does when she comes here is weep. She's been precisely twice since the baby was born. It was *Anna Karenina* all over again, the lost mother reunited with her son – and me of course in the role of Karenin. The whole scene took place because I'd had a word with one of the girls at the post office, a girl about my age, and told them that if So-and-So appeared they weren't to let her lay hands on Tima's money, so on the day her alimony was due my daughter appears in a white rage on the doorstep pushing a red pram before her ('So we've got a girl now' flashes through my mind) and looking all spotty again like she used to be when she was feeding Tima, a great fat female, all breast and shrieks, and starts yelling 'Get Tima ready, he's coming back to his f . . . g mother'. So then Tima started wailing in his thin little voice, like a puppy, and I calmly went and told her she should be deprived of her maternal rights – how could she go and dump her child on a frail old woman, etcetera etcetera. 'Come on Tima, you'll go mad living with this old bag,' says she, whereupon Tima starts yelping and squealing and I just stand there smiling calmly; yes, I say, yes, for the sake of fifty roubles you'd gladly have the child sent to the madhouse; look who's talking, says she, it's you who went and dumped your mother in the loony bin. 'And for your sake I did it,' I said, 'because of what you'd done' – nodding in the direction of Tima who's meanwhile standing there squealing like a piglet, eyes full of tears, refusing to come either to me or to his 'f . . . . g mother', just stands there rocking to and fro. I'll never forget the way he looked then, barely able to stand, a little child shaking from grief. As for the creature in the pram, her bastard daughter, she wakes up too and starts shrieking for good measure, and my great busty broad-shouldered daughter ups and yells too: You don't even want to look at your very own grand-daughter, and this is all I've got for her, this is the whole lot! Amid the shrieks she starts counting up all the money she lives on. You're nice and cosy here, aren't you? she says, while she's got nowhere! Nowhere! So I just smile sweetly and get right down to the point: Let him pay up, I said, the nice gentle-man who did his business and vanished into thin air, this is the second time it's happened, isn't it, no one can bear to live with you. Whereupon this maternal little daughter of mine whips the cloth off the table and hurls it a couple of yards in my direction, but fortunately you can't kill someone with a tablecloth. I calmly peeled it off my face and that was it. It was just a plastic cloth with nothing on it, no glass or crumbs or anything weighty like an iron.

This was our critical period, just before I got my pension; I get it two days after her alimony comes in. And my daughter says with a smirk that I shouldn't be getting the alimony, it didn't go on Tima but on other things – what other things? I threw my arms in the air – Look what we've got in the house, half a loaf of black bread and a drop of old soup! Take a look yourself, I yelled, wondering if there was any way she could have got wind that I'd used a bit of my money to buy some tablets for a certain person, code-named Friend – he'd come up to me once at the entrance to Central Pharmacy, a handsome, doleful-looking fellow, past his prime, his puffy face barely visible in the darkness: 'Help me, sister,' he said, 'my horse is dying.' His horse? What horse? So he told me he was a jockey and his favourite horse was dying, and at these words he ground his teeth and gripped me heavily by the shoulder, I was nailed to the spot by the weight of his hand. Ah the force of a man's hand! – at his bidding it can push you down, pull you up, pin you to the spot. But in the pharmacy, he said, they wouldn't accept a prescription for a horse, wouldn't give him the dose he needed, they'd sent him off to the veterinary pharmacy but it was closed. And the horse was dying. He needed at least to get hold of some painkillers but they'd only give him the tiniest dose, he needed my help. So idiot that I am I rushed as if hypnotised back up to the second floor and managed somehow to persuade the young sales-girl there to give me thirty tablets (for my three children, grandchildren, they were all lying sick at home it was evening I couldn't get a doctor till tomorrow and tomorrow there mightn't be any painkillers left etcetera etcetera) – and paid for them with my own money. They weren't that expensive, but the fact is our Friend never paid me back, I wrote

15

down my address for him and I'm still waiting for him to come. What a look there was in his eyes – he was blinking back the tears as he leant over to kiss my hand. It smelled of cooking oil: afterwards I kissed it myself on purpose and it really did stink of oil – but what can you do, my skin gets so rough and my fingers all chapped and blotchy.

I've reached the stage, alas, when you have to keep a careful watch on yourself but all I've got in the house is cooking oil, a poor substitute for those creams that you can't get for love or money these days! And try and make yourself beautiful without!

So enough of that horse, especially as when I put those three packets of tablets into that eager, prehensile, swollen hand, a grotesque-looking vampire with huge ears suddenly emerged out of nowhere, a silent mournful creature with a kind of hangdog look – just loomed up behind us on unsteady feet while we were conversing and my Friend was manfully attempting to write my address on a matchbox (I lent him my pen). My Friend simply brushed the vampire aside, carefully noting the address while the vampire danced around behind him, and then with a last kiss on the cooking oil he said farewell – for the horse's sake, he said, he had to go. There and then they divided up one pack of ten between them, huddled over it and gobbled up the tablets straight from the packet. Very odd people – how can you go taking a horse-size dose even supposing you've got a fever! No doubt the pair of them really were ill themselves. But were those miserable tablets they'd wangled out of me ever meant for a horse at all? Or was it deception pure and simple? Well, it will all be explained one fine day when my Friend comes round and rings on my doorbell at last.

So I yelled at her: Look for yourself, what could I have spent your money on? – and suddenly she goes into floods of tears and says: on Andrei, as always. She really was weeping from jealousy, just like in childhood. Well, well, I said, come and have a bite to eat, let's all have a bite. I sat her down, and Tima sat down too, and between us we finished off the last food in the house, and finally my daughter decided to cough up and gave us a bit of the money. Hurrah. Tima meanwhile never once went near the pram, and Alyona disappeared with the baby into my room and there among the books and manuscripts unwrapped the bastard and fed it. I looked through a chink – the child was hideous, nothing in her from our side, completely bald with bloated little eyes, fat all over and the strangest way of crying, not normal at all. Tima stood behind me and kept tugging at me to come away.

The child obviously took after the Deputy Director who had evidently fathered it, as I gathered from the relevant bits in Alyona's diary. She'd gone and hidden it, of all places, under a box on top of the bookcase! I do dust there from time to time though I must admit she'd hidden it so cleverly that it was only when I was looking for some old notebooks of mine that I was forced to get the whole lot down and have a proper sort-out. God knows how long it'd been lying there. Every time she turned up she'd start anxiously combing through the bookshelves – I was worried she was planning to steal my books and sell them, but clearly that wasn't it. Here are a few pages that made my heart sink:

*I beg that no one read this diary even after my death. Oh God, what filth, what utter filth have I plunged into, Lord forgive me. I've fallen so low. Yesterday I'd fallen so terribly low that I cried all morning. It's so terrible when morning comes, so painful to get up for the first time in your life from someone else's bed, to put on yesterday's underwear again, I rolled my knickers into a little ball and just put on my tights and went into the bathroom. He even said 'Why so shy all of a sudden?' Why indeed. Because yesterday I'd felt so at home with his powerful odour, his smooth skin, his hard muscles, his bursting veins, his animal coat all bedewed with sweat, his body like a beast's, a gorilla's, a horse's – but in the morning all this became alien and repulsive the moment he said he was very sorry but he had business to do by ten in the morning and he had to leave. So I said I had to be somewhere by eleven too, shame, shame, I burst into tears and ran into the bathroom and wept. I wept under the shower, washing out my knickers and washing my whole body which had suddenly become alien too, as if I were watching myself in a pornographic movie, my stranger's body where at that very moment some kind of chemical reaction was taking place, I was filled with seething slime, everything was swollen and sore and burning, something was going on that needed to be nipped in the bud, stopped, crushed, or I was going to die.* [We'd see all too clearly nine months later what precisely was going on.– A.A.]

*I stood there under the shower, my mind gone blank, and thought: So that's it! He doesn't need me any more. What am I to do with myself? The whole of my life up till now has turned to ashes. I can no longer live without him, but he doesn't need me. All that remains is to throw myself under a train.* [A lovely man she'd found to do it

18

for. – A.A.] *What am I doing here? He's leaving already.
To add to it all I'd phoned M.*[that's me – A.A.]
*yesterday evening as soon as I'd got there to say I was going
to stay the night at Lena's, and Mum started yelling
something uplifting along the lines of 'Lena my foot, you
can stay at your Lena's for good for all I care'* [What I'd
in fact said was: 'How can you, darling, your child is
ill, you're his mother, how can you?' and so on, but
in her haste she just said 'Okay, fine, 'bye' and hung
up on me just as I was saying 'I don't see what's fine
about it'. – A.A.] *I hung up and smiled brightly so he
wouldn't guess anything, he was pouring out the wine at
the coffee table and suddenly sort of froze, obviously struck
by some particular thought. And then he seemed to make up
his mind about something – I could see it written all over
his face. Maybe I'd been too upfront saying I was going to
spend the night with him, maybe I shouldn't have said
that, but I'd said it precisely with a sense of self-sacrifice, a
feeling that I was giving my whole self to him, fool that I
was.* [precisely – A.A.] *He stood there stonily with the
bottle in his hand, and I was already past caring. It wasn't
that I'd lost control of myself, I'd known right from the
beginning that I was going to go with this man and do
whatever he wanted. All I knew about him was that he was
the Deputy Director of Academic Affairs, I'd seen him at
meetings and that was it. Nothing like this could have
remotely occurred to me before, I was completely shaken
when he came up to my table in the canteen and sat down
next to me without so much as a glance, let alone hello, a
big man miles older than me. His friend came and sat
down too, a terrific talker, bit of a windbag, with a great
head of hair and hardly any beard, he was forever
preening his pale wispy moustache, had the face of a film*

19

*star in a police film but looked thoroughly camp, the lab
assistants said he was completely weird, in the middle of
doing it he was apt to jump up at the crucial moment and
rush into a corner crying 'Don't look at me!' What it all
meant they couldn't explain, didn't know themselves.
Anyway this chatterbox immediately started talking to me
while the man next to me kept silent – then suddenly trod
on my foot . . .* [Note: My God, what kind of creature
have I brought up! Enough to turn your hair grey
overnight! It was that very evening, I remember, that
Tima suddenly developed a strange cough, I woke
up and he was barking away: Khukh! Khukh! and he
couldn't breathe properly, he kept gasping and
gasping and screwing himself in a knot, he'd gone
all grey, all the breath had left him and he couldn't
breathe in at all, he was turning blue, kept coughing
and coughing and started crying from fright. Well
I'd been through all this before, it wasn't the first
time, he'd got a form of croup, a swollen larynx and
very bad pharyngitis, I'd been through it all before
with the children and the first thing you've got to do
is get the child seated and calm them down, get their
feet into hot water and mustard and then call the
emergency doctor, but you can't do all this at once,
you can never get through to emergencies first go
and you have to have someone else there with you to
help. Meanwhile look what this someone else was
up to.] *The man next to me suddenly trod on my foot.
Then he did it a second time, still not looking at me, still
buried in his cup of coffee, but smiling by now. The blood
rushed to my head and I went all faint. It was two years
since I'd divorced Sasha, not that long a time, but no one
realised we'd never really been man and wife! We slept in*

20

*the same bed, but he never touched me!* [My commentary:
All this is nonsense. Anyway I got the situation under
control, sat the child down, stroked his hands, gradually got him to breathe through his nose, gently
gently now, there we are, through your little nosey
darling, that's the way, try not to cry sweetheart, but
if only there'd been someone else there to heat the
water! I carried him into the bathroom, turned the
hot tap on full blast, it was literally boiling, we started breathing in the steam, both of us soaked with
sweat, and little by little the cough began to ease. My
little sunshine! Always and everywhere it's been just
you and me and that's the way it's going to stay! A
woman's always weak and indecisive over things that
concern her alone, but she's a wild beast when it
comes to her children! But what was his mother writing meanwhile? – A.A.] *We slept in the same bed, but he
never touched me! I didn't know a thing then.*
[Commentary: a good-for-nothing bastard he was,
the swine!! – A.A. ] *I didn't know anything, hadn't a
clue, I was even grateful to him for not touching me, the
baby made me so tired, my back ached from bending over
Tima the whole time, for two months I'd been bleeding non-
stop and I couldn't ask any of my friends about it, none of
them had had babies yet. I was the first and thought it was
normal* – [Commentary: how silly can you get? If
you'd only told your mother about it I'd have told
you straight out, the bastard was simply terrified
she'd get pregnant again! – A.A.] – *I thought that was
how it had to be, that in my condition you shouldn't do it
and so on. He simply shared my bed, ate* [no comment
needed there – A.A. ]

*drank tea* [belched, peed, picked his nose – A.A.]

*shaved* [his favourite occupation – A.A.]

*read, did his assignments and wrote up his lab notes, slept again and gently snored, and I loved him tenderly and devotedly and was ready to kiss his feet – for what did I know about life? What did I know?* [Go on, go on, make our hearts bleed. – A.A.] *It had only ever happened to me once, that first time, when he suggested we go for a walk one evening after supper; it was still midsummer, the time of white nights, we walked and walked and then went into the hayloft, but why did he choose me? That afternoon we were working in the fields digging potatoes and he said: 'Are you free this evening?', and I said: 'I don't know', we were working the same patch, he had the fork and I trailed along behind him in my rough gloves. The sun was shining. Suddenly my friend Lena shouted out 'Watch out, Alyona!' I glanced round and there right next to me stood a dog with his eyes screwed up and something revolting sticking out from under his belly.* [That's what comes of sending young girls out to work on the farms. – A.A.] *I jumped back and Sasha waved his fork threateningly at the dog. In the evening we went to the hayloft, he climbed up first and gave me his hand – oh, that hand of his! I flew up like a feather. And then we sat there like a pair of fools, I kept on moving his hand away and saying please don't. Then suddenly something rustled right next to us, he grabbed me and pushed me down and both of us froze. He was shielding me with his body as if from gunfire, making sure no one could see me. He defended me as he would his own child. It felt so good, so warm and close, I snuggled up to him, this is it, this is love, I thought, I couldn't tear myself away. Whatever was rustling – he said it was mice – I no longer cared. He told me it wouldn't hurt the next time, don't*

22

*shout, he said, be quiet, you have to be strong, he was*
*certainly being strong, and I just pressed up against him*
*with every fibre of my being. He thrust himself into the*
*bloody mess, the bloody shreds of my body like a pump,*
*pumping my blood, the straw underneath me was wet,*
*I was squeaking like a rubber toy with a hole in its bottom,*
*and I was thinking: in one night he's gone and tried every-*
*thing he's ever read about and heard about from the others*
*in the hostel, but I didn't care, I loved him and pitied him*
*like my own little son and feared only that he'd leave me,*
*he was quite worn out.*

[If only she'd been like that with her actual son!
Words fail me. – A.A.]

*When it was all over he said there was nothing more*
*beautiful than woman. And I couldn't tear myself away*
*from him, I kept stroking his shoulders and arms and belly,*
*he sobbed and pressed against me again, and already it felt*
*completely different, as if we'd found each other again after*
*a long separation, we didn't hurry this time, I was learning*
*to respond to him, I knew that I was leading him in the right*
*direction, he was trying and trying for something and at last*
*he got there, and I fell silent, and that was it.*

[Full stop! And the poor spinster schoolmarm was
given a harpsichord, to quote the Japanese *haiku*.
Oh children, children, you grow 'em and feed 'em,
live and put up with 'em, in the words of that old
cleaning lady at the holiday resort – she was busy
destroying a dove's nest so the birds wouldn't shit on
the porch, she poked her stick in and whacked it
and one little fledgeling, quite a sizeable one, fell
straight out of the nest.]

*My heart was pounding away, and I knew he had hit*
*the right spot*

[poke, poke]

*orgasm, that's what it's called*

[and as the poet Dobrynin's son put it to me once on the phone when he was drunk, breathing heavily as if from a fight, can you really call someone human when they've been screwed to pieces like a piece of old bast – I don't know who he had in mind.]

*– I beg that no one read this.*

[Don't read it, children. There'll be time enough when you grow up. – A.A. ]

*And then he started thrusting harder, lay on top and pressed himself to me, moaned and made a strange hissing noise,* sss-sss *between his teeth, shook his head wildly and said . . . I love you.* [Complete depravity from the point of view of any decent person. – A.A.] *Afterwards he lay spread out in the pale morning light, and I got up feeling like an empty shell, trembling all over, my legs like cotton wool, and started trying to gather up my things. My slip had got in a twist underneath me and was drenched in blood. I covered up all the wet bloodied hay, climbed down and tottered over to the pond to wash out my slip, and he traipsed after me all naked and bloody; we washed one another and flopped about in the pond, swam around for ages and splashed in the translucent brownish water, warm as milk. And that was when we were spotted by Veronica, self-disciplined Veronica, always first up in the morning and out first thing to wash and clean her teeth, she spotted my bloody slip, still unwashed, lying there on the bank and squeaked in fright, Sasha dived straight into the water, Veronica looked at us both wild-eyed and took to her heels, and I rushed to wash out the slip while Sasha hastily threw on his dry things and fled. I think he was frightened off for ever by that moment. And that was it.*

24

*After that he never came near me again.* [Yes, and as a result of this horror and depravity little Tima was born, darling beautiful innocent Tima. Who says that only real love makes beautiful children? Tima, despite all, is lovely as the gods – despite this disgraceful, shameful beginning. May these pages stay hidden from those children's eyes! Let them find out later who's who, let them learn sometime who their mother is and who I am, but later! I must put all this stuff back on the bookcase, she'll dig it out anyway, one of these days she'll remember, all this time she'd been searching like a maniac for that diary of hers, she'd die if she found out, but for now at least she's safely out of the way. I'm writing all this for her sake too, so that she too should understand who's led what sort of life! Yes! I, for instance, never suffered any pain from a man, never! All this stuff about pain is an illusion. And I'll take my reflections a bit further. Here's what happens: out of all these tears and groans and blood a tiny little cell is born, one cell in the spawn, a tiny tadpole, that's the result of this explosion, this eruption, one little creature happens to be the first to swim in on the waves and take root, and that applies to all of us, that's how we all began! Ah, Nature, what tricks She plays on us! How great She is! Why does She wring from us all these sufferings, this horror, blood, stench, sweat, slime, convulsions, love, violence, pain, sleepless nights, hard labour – apparently just so that all should be well in the end! But alas! In the end the whole thing turns sour again. – A.A.]

*I stood under the shower sobbing my heart out, there in the home of the Deputy Director, a serious bespectacled man,*

*and all of a sudden he comes in, climbs right into the bath
with me, I barely had time to flip my knickers up over the
shower curtain. He wiped my eyes, he looked at me, moved
back a little, squatting down, breathing heavily – you have
to go – no, no, just hold on – you'll miss the train – silence,
hot water streaming down – if only it could be like this for
ever, how can I live without you, leave me, go, what are you
doing, you'll be late.*

[No, this really should be left for posterity, com-
pared with her I'm just I don't know what, an innocent babe, even though this was only her second
man: those hounds sniff out her female weakness
straight away – her readiness to fall flat on her back
right there and then from happiness. – A.A.]

*He got me dressed, dried my hair with the hair dryer, and
I started weeping all over again, feverish tears, as if I were
saying goodbye to my father, it was just like when Dad left
us for good and I clung to his knees, and my mother in a
mad fury dragged me away, smiling all the while and saying 'What are you crying for, girl, he's not worth it – and
you, get out, don't you dare set foot . . . ' etcetera, etcetera.*
[A fine comparison to make, her own father com-
pared with this . . . with the father of that bastard
Katya. – A.A. ] *'Don't cry,' he said. 'I'll come and find you
again, write to me poste restante, I always get my mail
that way, don't lose touch' – he kept mumbling away, fussing about in the apartment, picking up bits of fluff and
dust, stripping the sheets off the bed, carefully putting on
new ones and then tossing around for a minute or two on
the bed to give the impression of a good night's solitary
sleep, and finally he gathered up all the stained bed linen,
carefully wrapped it up in a sheet of newspaper, stuffed it
in a bag and handed it to me. 'What's this?' – 'You wash*

*them.' – 'And then?'* He thought a moment and said *'Get them back to me. Standard procedure.'* [Of course he wouldn't have dreamt of saying 'You keep them' – no way. No, no, she was to give them a thorough scrub and boil-up, iron them out nicely and – would you believe it! – hand them back to him! She did the right thing – men like that can't bear the slightest material loss! And in fact it would have been improper on his part, I suppose, he was right not to say 'You keep them' – how could he make her a present like that after meeting just once?! But he might have just chucked them in the bin outside – or was he too mean? – A.A.]

*As we were leaving he looked regretfully at his watch and at his marital bed, it was obvious he wanted to make use of every minute and was casting around for some pretext to start undoing all my clothes again. In the end he didn't need to undo anything, he managed to do it almost fully dressed, he just kept saying: 'Hold on, hold on, just a second.' It was all very simple, I put my tights back on again and he said: 'You go up one floor and call the lift, I'll go down on foot.' When I came out the front door he'd already driven off in his car or caught a taxi – at any rate vanished into thin air, there were several people waiting for the Sunday bus at the bus stop, but he wasn't among them. It was only once I was in the Metro I realised that I'd left my wet knickers draped over the shower curtain! Horror!* [She knew very well what she was doing, no doubt the minute the wife came home she'd chuck her husband out, slap him in the face with that nice wet pair of knickers! Straight on his glasses! And he knew just what he was up to as well, it would have been a shame to let her go scot-free after all so he

27

just kept pumping away at her right up to the last
minute, and fully clad at that! Why don't you value
yourself at all, why can't you just say 'No'? – A.A.]

*My hair literally stood on end from horror, I pictured his
wife climbing into the bath, drawing the shower curtain
and smack! My wet knickers land on her head like a gift
from God! I was dying of shame all the way home, and
tonight sitting here I'd like to sink through the floor! My
heart sinks to my boots every time I think of it. Everything
I care for betrayed and desecrated! The way he looked at me
that time in the canteen, sideways, shiftily, and then deliberately, carefully pressed his foot on mine, pressed hard,
and then for good measure put his hand on my knee and
started running a finger up a bit higher, but he didn't get
where he was planning to, I clamped right up and removed
his hand. He and his friend escorted me gallantly right to
my door, then suddenly he said to his companion: 'I'll ring
you later, I need to have a quick word here . . . ' whereupon
his companion bends his feminine head in a half bow and,
smiling significantly, sails off down the corridor. And the
Deputy Director scribbles down his address, the date and the
time on a page from his notepad and hands it to me. I went
and met him that very evening. And felt so happy! On my
way there I felt so happy! And look how stupidly and
shamefully it ended!'*

[End of diary.]


But in fact that was only the beginning. Soon after
all this Tima and I virtually lost sight of our young
mother (she was just twenty-two at the time), she
was doing her finals at the institute, she'd finished
her pre-diploma practicals (she was supposed to be

working for her diploma at the institute where he was Deputy Director, but all her free time was spent with him – a middle-aged man, thirty-seven years old, what a joke!), she thought of nothing else. But then came the real ending. She turns up one day: 'I have to talk to you' – so do I, incidentally – 'I'm going to get married.' Oh yes, so what's the story, how many wives is he planning to have? You can't be married to everyone at once. 'You don't understand, Mum.' What, has he left his wife then? – '*Mum*, that's not the point.' Oh I see, you're going to be the mistress of a married man. 'How can you be so stupid, Mum, we're going to have a baby, and he's going to get us an apartment.' 'Us' means you, does it? And what about him? 'Mum! I can't bring him home here to you! And I won't be taking you there either' – she said suddenly, with that inveterate hatred in her voice – 'I'll come and get Tima, but I'm not taking you! Never!'

She didn't take me with her. But she collected the alimony. Not straight away, it's true. It was only when she realised he was a complete skinflint, a stingy bastard who'd never dream of squandering his money on her. Love in these people's cases is always very lofty and platonic – i.e. they're never prepared to pay for anything. Their love is entirely spiritual, because their need for money is always greater than anyone else's. Spoil the ship for a ha'p'orth of tar, that's the kind of people we're talking about! They've always got some plan on the go, be it a car or a computer or a video camera; they spend their whole lives saving up for something and love 'getting married' for free on the side, think they've paid a woman in hard currency just by sticking their thing inside her.

So this is who we've been paying for, this is the person we've been supporting. My poor beggar of a daughter – ow ow!

Night. The kid's asleep. I keep up my defences, though every now and then my daughter delivers a new blow: just before New Year – I'll never forget this – Tima and I were planning to spend it at home, as usual no one had invited us anywhere, we went to the Christmas tree market and gathered up a bouquet of the bushiest fan-shaped branches, just like a tree! Then we made some little flags and animals out of coloured paper from old magazines, and at that point Alyona shows up, supposedly to wish us happy New Year; she'd bought Tima a blue plastic cat of surpassing ugliness but Tima made a great fuss of it, tucked it up in bed, and I didn't tell the poor child that his own mother, completely brazen, had stolen from her own family home two boxes of Christmas tree decorations, leaving us only three. I wept. But she forgot about the electric garland! So for New Year our fir bouquet was bedecked from head to foot, with my sixth sense I'd kept hidden from Alyona the little glass house with the flashing roof and two windows in the sides. Tima loves looking in at the windows, it's just like the sugar house in *The Bluebird*. I lit up the garland for just a while, the little house twinkled, and Tima and I (together with that hideous plastic monster) did a dance round the tree, and silently I wiped away my tears.

And for New Year too we gave each other presents: Tima wrapped up a picture he'd painted in a bit of newspaper, and I made a very decent little doll out of rags, a glove puppet, good for play acting. He's got four of these dolls now. I don't find it easy making them, it's hard to get their faces looking nice, there's always a problem with the nose, so now I just put in a sort of comma. But I can't always glue and cut and sew things for him, he always wants to do it himself and get it right straight away, but he tires so quickly! After ten minutes he starts grizzling, he's still very small and not very dexterous yet, he keeps doing it wrong and gets in a mess and starts tugging crossly at the thing. And I'm busy, I have to get on with my work! And then he starts grimacing. It's his nervous tic.

I tried to make a present for Andrei as well, I put together a little book entitled 'The rules of *bon ton*', a sort of brochure, but he rejected it and started demanding his usual price, twenty-five roubles, crudely over the telephone. I'd put a lot of work into this text, emphasising in bold certain principles of so-called family behaviour. Andrei, incidentally, is threatening once again to throw himself out the window.

It's true he said this to his wife, not me – God knows how she'd gone and offended him this time, the last time he didn't even issue threats, he simply couldn't stand it and really did throw himself out of the second-floor window in a state of extreme intoxication, as they diagnosed at the hospital. He broke both legs, falling badly on the asphalt. He had to stay in hospital and now he has problems with his heel.

It hurts unbearably, so his wife says, but you can't actually see anything. Some nerve or other in the heel has been crushed. Now he's incapable of doing work that involves either walking or standing, he can only work sitting down. In fact the only thing he's fit for, the only thing that would give him a chance to lie down from time to time as well, is working as a watchman of some kind. It's a tragedy, a tragedy! It's five years now since it happened. Both legs, five years ago, from a second-floor window.


I'm scared of both of them, husband and wife. She said on the phone that everything was okay, yesterday he tore the sleeve off her dressing-gown but otherwise things are okay. She's a nurse. It's hard work, of course, but she gives him his injections, painkillers, massages, footbaths. Imagine it at his age – still a young man! But then look at Alyona, two years younger than him – I said to her when we had our last scene from *Anna Karenina*, the meeting with the long-lost son, we were sitting over our bowl of soup and I said: You should keep a better watch on yourself, look what's become of you! She looked away and her eyes filled with tears, she was seething with hatred for me again. She got up without so much as a 'thank you' or 'piss off', not even a word to Tima, and off she sails with her fat baby in the pram. She had to drag it all the way downstairs on foot, four floors, it's such a curse not having a lift.

*

The jealousy started when she was a child and then seemed to pass, later on when they were teenagers they even used to talk to each other at nights in the kitchen, shutting me out when I would have been so happy to listen to their chatter. I'd leave my door half open, but alas! The kitchen was sealed as firmly as their hearts. Then when Andrei was in prison she even used to write to him, more of that anon. That was before she brought home that oaf who didn't know how to sit down or stand up properly and gobbled up everything in the fridge without thinking. Straight from darkest Ternopol, what can you expect. He used to go into ecstasies shaving, it was a half-hour session every morning in front of the mirror caressing himself with his electric razor, transcendental meditation by the bathroom basin. He'd stand there with his eyes half-closed, and when things got urgent and you poked your head round the door his mind had clearly wandered off completely, Tima would be howling, wet through, while my dear daughter went into labour every morning on the lavatory and Andrei, just home from prison, couldn't get a foot in anywhere, bath and toilet were always fully occupied when he got up in the morning, he'd sit there like a caged beast in the kitchen where he had his folding bed and drive me away so he could drink his coffee alone. The bitterest cup of coffee. It was a year later he jumped, but that was already from his wife's place, not from our overcrowded apartment. To be honest that was what put an end to his past as a hoodlum, doing his time in prison for getting in a fight when other young men were serving in the army. Love, love, love, plain love

33

and pity were all I felt for him when he got out. I stood waiting for him at one entrance to Butyrka prison and he came out the other, just as he was, I'd brought him fresh clean clothes but I was waiting at the other entrance so he walked out just as he was and crossed the whole of Moscow on bus and trolley without paying – he didn't have a kopeck on him of course – and then there was still quite a way to go on foot. Having confused the two entrances and messed up the meeting, I waited a while in vain and then rushed back home, and there he was sitting there, just twenty years old, still in his prison uniform. He'd even got his queer's cap, as he called it, pointing to the thing lying on the table. Everything the colour of coal. And this was spring, the streets were full, everyone must have been looking at him. He looked quite the hero, all gaunt and drawn, I squatted down and took his boots off for him. And then he asked quietly: 'Who is he? What's going on?' At this point our oaf-cum-cretin comes out, he'd been asleep, they didn't know day from night that pair, and Tima started squawking. That's what you've come home to, my son. Tima didn't sleep with me at nights, I can never sleep properly, and he didn't get a wink in the daytime either when they were home though both of them slept. Being a poet I'm always at home no matter what. But this one time I hadn't been there, and Ternopol himself had opened the door to Andrei. What questions were asked I've no idea. But Andrei still went on: 'Who is he? What's going on?', realising I'd somehow acquired another son (Ternopol). So I started explaining everything, told him we hadn't written because we didn't want to worry him.

I wish I hadn't had to come back here at all, says Andrei, I'll only wind up with another sentence anyway, I've had it, he says, I couldn't care less what happens now. I'd been explaining the whole thing to him, told him right away who this character was and what it had cost us to to get him married to Alyona. Ternopol meanwhile slipped past the kitchen, all swollen from sleep, disappeared into the lavatory and started rattling the bolt, it doesn't close properly and anyway why bother, we're all family after all. All we need do is say 'Anyone in there?'; the lock doesn't work in any case, it's obviously got rusty with no one using it. But he'd rattle away at it like a frightened rabbit. He hadn't known either what kind of family he was coming into and what skeletons we kept in the cupboard, we'd only got him married by a whisker and he hadn't even got himself registered yet. It was only with others' help I'd got him married at all, I'd had to turn to the other girls who'd been with them at the collective farm potato-picking, a right bunch they were too. Tima was born in June and Andrei turned up just over a fortnight later. Pure Sodom in our house; I could see it all begin. What had he been through, my one and only beloved and suffering son? His muscles wasted, his puppy fat all gone, his plump lips compressed – he looked a real picture, couldn't take your eyes off him. And all in a get-up the colour of asphalt.

The situation was as follows: we got Ternopol married by the skin of our teeth, the college authorities gave him a warning: if he didn't go ahead he'd be in deep trouble, might even end up doing his army service. We finally got him when she was close to her eighth month, that poor little sufferer brought him home, Alyona, my permanent heartache. He arrived with a look that said We are displeased, We being His Majesty the Emperor of All Russia and the town of Ternopol in particular. So His Majesty was seated and sat there motionless, never graced us with a single glance, and Alyona was all swollen up, so young, she looked dreadful, great hollows under her eyes, her lips bluish, her hair all lank. I've never let myself go like that, no matter what happened I've always looked after my hair. Hair is so important, it's such an asset to have well-washed, well-groomed hair! And preferably nice fresh skin as well, but that comes from plenty of walking in the fresh air; once upon a time I used to love to take a stroll but I never have time for it these days, just dash from one place to the other.

'When I was pregnant with you, Alyona,' I told her, 'I didn't let myself go. Get a grip on yourself, go and wash your hair. What's the matter with you – can't be the first time you've gone and got yourself pregnant, surely? Why go into mourning?'

Alyona: 'Did I warn you, sweetheart, my mother's a total idiot?'

Even he looked aghast, but you could see he was a tough young customer, clearly believed in himself and his own strength.

So they went and sat in the other room, what used to be the children's room, and settled in, and she brought him something to eat. They ate some salad, a spring salad – just potatoes and onion and mayonnaise – then a whole tub of soup, and then they ate up the last three meatballs I'd managed to cobble together, thank God, with a bit of bread to flesh them out. I'd been saving up for Andrei's homecoming, I'd even economised on poor Alyona, let alone myself. I can live on nothing at all, a cup of tea's enough to make me fat, such times we're living through. He (His Majesty) gobbled up the three meatballs, I don't think there was anything left for Alyona. I gave her my portion in the kitchen, had a quiet word with her while he wasn't there:

'The young man's got quite an appetite, has he? Then you eat up mine.'

She stood ever so still and looked at me, quite pale all of a sudden, and out of the blue burst into tears:

'I ha-a-te you! God how I ha-a-ate you!'

'Now what's all this about? The young man's hungry, I quite understand. But you need something as well if you're eating for two. And by the way, is he going to be bringing in some money for food or simply eating up all of yours? You know yourself how much I earn, a poet isn't paid big money.'

'Scribbler' was all she had to say, my Alyona.

Same old story.


And all this while – little did I know! – it was darling Tima she was carrying inside her, Tima in honour of some Ternopol ancestor. Oh if I'd known I would have carried her round in my own arms, but all I could think of then was how on earth to feed her and the little one and on top of it all this husband

37

hung round our necks, washed up on our doorstep the devil knows how, the coward, he was so scared he'd be expelled and sent to the army if he didn't get married, terrified they'd turn him into a queer because of his good looks, but what about Andrei then, I ask you, what had he been through in the camps? What on earth had he been through? What mockeries was he made to suffer, I ask you, and how can I ever make up for it all if you go eating and drinking every last ounce I have?

But there we were, fixed up with a husband; they settled into the children's room and we got two girls in for witnesses – not the ones that had been at the farm, apparently he didn't want any more of them. I made a potato salad, meat with macaroni and a pie with dried fruit. In the morning, the minute she woke up, she darted into the kitchen before I had a chance and made an omelette from the last three eggs, obviously for that beloved husband of hers. No doubt she stood over him with a napkin on her arm like his devoted servant. Later I said to her:

'It's all very well you becoming his servant, the fact is there were three eggs left here for the two of us and I'd been planning on making pancakes. There's not a thing left in the house to eat. Let him pay thirty roubles at least, it's downright dishonourable to get married just for food. What we eat in the mornings is porridge made with water. How are you going to feed the baby, what'll you have to feed him on, a dried-up breast? Dried up!'

I wanted to hug her and have a good cry, but she jumped right away from me. And that was the way it carried on with us. She was using up her last ounce

to please her darling – that's what she called him –
and after a while I just stayed all the time in my
room. I turned the fridge off – why waste electricity
for a start, and anyway I just didn't see how else I
could react, a mother, insulted, rejected, left on my
own, when I'd dragged home two full bags of shop-
ping after a whole day's queuing and then – 'a hungry guest turned up and ate it all' (to use her happy
phrase). Those guests certainly didn't let the grass
grow green on the path to our house, all of them
were so moved by the situation of these starving
newlywed parents-to-be. She of course behaved
majestically, queening it in the kitchen over His
Majesty's potatoes, His Majesty's three ounces of
butter, His Majesty's sausage; delicious smells came
wafting out and it got to the point where they even
carted off my only kettle and I meanwhile, starving
myself in preparation, waiting for my one and only
beloved son to come back, scrimping and saving on
everything, was reduced to boiling up water in a
saucepan, just plain water; bread and tea was all I
had for breakfast lunch and dinner, prisoners' fare.
Since that was all he had, that was all I'd have too.

'My mother's completely bonkers' – that was how
she explained to her guests my forays in and out of
the kitchen with a saucepanful of boiling water.


I never said hello to any of them. But it seemed my
hatred towards His Majesty had somehow united
them, if feebly, as a family. They enjoyed making fun
of me. She'd perform her solo with him as accom-
panist – in other words they'd put on a great show at

my expense, and it's true my only dream was that the pair of them would simply clear off and leave the children's room for Andrei. But where could they go? Where? I told them I wasn't going to register the husband at our place, because that way they'd get a family room in a hostel much more quickly, where-upon a great storm broke out in the house with floods of tears from Alyona. Aha, I said, so that's it, is it, he went and got married just so as to get his residence permit, did he? In that case let him get unmarried again quickly. So Alyona had a good think and decided on her strategy: at his instigation she announced that in that case she would veto Andrei's permit when he came out of prison, she had the right to do that. Ouch! That was below the belt. So as usual after a major set-to we all disap-peared to our respective corners to calm down, and in due course she emerged and came into my room. I was sitting there shaking, supposedly at work.

'Do you wish me dead, is that it?' she asked, burst-ing into tears (once again).

'Why should I wish you dead, go and live as you please with your future offspring. But if your sole aim in setting up family is to get him his residence permit, you might at least pause to think is it hon-estly worth it? Is it worth the sacrifice of our whole family – Andrei without a roof over his head, my mother languishing in mental hospital . . . ?'

She'd cry at nothing at all in those days, the tears simply streamed from her wide-open eyes, those clear bright eyes of hers – what have they done to me, those dear eyes, what have the lot of you done to me!

I longed to give her a hug, and oddly enough she didn't resist this time. With my hand on her shoulder – such delicate shoulders she has – I could feel her trembling.

'All right,' she says, 'I know you don't need me, me and the baby, all you ever need is your criminal son. That's it, isn't it? Do you want me to go and die? Or are you just hoping the baby'll somehow evaporate, is that it? Well, I'm telling you now, the baby's there to stay. And I'm warning you, if anything happens to my darling, that beloved Andrei of yours is going to be put away for much, much longer.'

That's all she could say about her brother, her poor suffering brother, who'd taken the blame on himself for the sins of eight others! About the brother she'd wept over at nights (I'd heard her), the brother she'd written to, long letters full of funny little details, she was too shy to let me read them (but I read them all the same and was delighted, she had real potential as a writer, I once said that to her and cited a phrase from one of those letters as proof, some little joke she'd made, but she went wild, accusing me of God knows what, I was the KGB, she was being searched – a dreadful, dreadful row we had over that). True, it was only for the first two months she'd wept over him; the remaining nine months she'd had reason enough to weep on her own account.

And now we were all waiting for the Victory Day amnesty on the 9th May!

'As if it weren't enough that you spy on us,' she

41

said quietly, 'spy on us and our friends and go calling the police – as if that weren't enough you have to go stealing Sasha's military service card! He was looking for it everywhere! It was driving him mad!'

'Oh yes?' I said, for a moment left quite speechless. 'I stole his military card? What the hell do you think I care about your Ternopol!'

'And two days later you put it back again on purpose!'

Paranoia and schizophrenia – it was a straightforward case of persecution mania. After that I spent my last money on a lock for my door and got a nice man to come and fit it. He charged me just one rouble and joked that he was looking for a wife. Silly man, he had no idea that I wasn't exactly young any more – me, about to be a grandmother! Oh the divine simplicity of ordinary folk who'll like a person for who they are, regardless of age or anything else. The following day he turned up with a box of chocolates and was greeted on the doorstep by my daughter demanding to know who he was (I was standing in the hall in my dressing-gown with the daisy design). He held out the box and offered me a chocolate. To judge by appearances he'd already given himself a treat or two of another kind. My daughter said demonstratively: 'Mum! What next!' and at these words my poor suitor, having girded his loins with a bit of Dutch courage, turned tail and disappeared for ever, or at any rate never set foot in our house again.

But after the door closed behind him my daughter burst out laughing.

'Well, well, Mum, there's a classic case if ever I saw one of someone on the lookout for a Moscow residence permit. You should be more careful, if you go catching some nasty disease or pubic lice I won't let you into the bathroom, let alone anywhere near my bonny baby . . . '

She wouldn't let me near my own darling Tima!

'. . . until you get yourself medically certified free of venereal disease.'

That was how she chose to express herself, all flushed with triumph.

'At the classes at the clinic they were warning everyone about syphilis and how you shouldn't ever drink from those glasses at the soda machines, and now into the bargain we've got you . . .' Of course she's the very model of respectability herself these days, a wife and expectant mother, sailing off to her lectures at the clinic with her nose in the air, such an example to us all.


I walked off, locked myself in my room and wept long and bitterly. I was still only fifty years old then! Ah, when I look back now on those vanished years of my youth, when my joints had barely begun to ache, my blood pressure was fine – I had everything then, everything! At nights, it's true, I was already suffering from insomnia, I'd fall asleep then wake again, fall asleep then wake. Then, like an avalanche, my life started slipping away . . . but we'll draw a veil over that, everyone has their secrets and many bear them to the grave, there are some things you can never ever divulge. You folk that are old and sick, I weep for you. When I think now of my youth in those days – how little I valued it then; I thought I had one foot in the grave already! Not that I let it get me down – I was forever planning to run up some new dress or skirt, I'd dash round looking for odds and ends of reduced stuff in the shops, I was full of dreams in those days, be it crocheting a lacy top out of some cheap thread or whatever. Amazing how you can live in the clouds like that while standing on the brink of tragedy! Fancy dreaming of lacy tops on the edge of that abyss, just before those two beloved beings turned up – Andrei and Tima!

These days I keep meaning to make something for Tima out of those scraps I managed to get hold of then, but I'm not up to doing shirts, and anyway Masha dear creature that she is gives us some of her boy's hand-me-downs, though nothing to write home about, no shoes or jackets or anything. Just odds and ends. And then of course there's the school uniform to think of. Still, somehow as always I'll scrape up the money for everything.

Whatever one may say about Masha she's all I have left, the past's the past and there' s no point going over it now, how all my former friends scattered one by one, disappeared into the bosom of their families after I'd lost my job – and it shouldn't have been me they sacked – now all that's left is the odd supposedly casual phone call on my part and us dropping in on them now and then to get fed, I'm careful it's never more than once every couple of months in each place. We've already been over all that and over the economies you have to make, but even in those days, before those two beloved creatures turned up, I was economising on everything I could. My dear young lodgers got their student grants and even some financial help from the union, not to mention those lunatic friends of theirs would now and then bring their own food with them just for the pleasure of their dear friends' company, and the ones that stayed overnight and tried to settle in with them on their floor (and that pair of fools were so moved by this demonstration of love, they positively encouraged these attempts at communal life) – these overnight visitors would sometimes end up feeding the whole crowd! I held my ground and caused no end of rows calling the police to protest against this bunch of strangers staying in my own home past eleven p.m.! Once a whole police squad came clattering up the stairs and thundered into the hallway, woke up our lodgers and all their nocturnal visitors and asked them to present their documents. That frightened off the pretenders and brought about a veritable downpour of animosity on the part of my daughter. His Majesty wouldn't even look in my direction, he was so terrified, never mind saying hello or goodbye. A Greek tragedy and no mistake! Andrei, Andrei, I pleaded in my heart, you must hold on, they'll have you arrested again for sure!

*

But I never wished them any harm, and seeing how poor they were I kept making pot after pot of porridge in the mornings with the oats I'd put by, supposedly for myself, it was good for my ailing liver, but the pot was always empty by the time I got to it (and of course left dirty as well). Sasha thank God hated porridge, had done ever since he was a child, it made him quite sick. Whereas my Alyona, praise be, couldn't get enough of it. Alas, I didn't manage to find out what else he hated, and in the meantime he made a clean sweep of whatever came to hand. But he couldn't touch my food. Whenever he was setting off to the library (it was the spring term, he'd take half the morning to get going, get shaved, get his hair brushed) I'd leave a bit of soup in the kitchen and fish for the main course and be left as usual with a pile of dirty dishes, but that was par for the course. How I loved that daughter of mine, her slender back, her grubby little pink heels as she slapped round in her tatty old slippers, that back of hers – she never showed me her face. Oh if I'd had my way I'd have bathed her and fed her properly, had her sleep between lovely clean sheets on fluffy pillows under the satin quilt (for the time being I'd put it safely away), she'd have stayed in bed all those days before her delivery, but as it was she kept running around, did her exams ahead of time, contrived to get hold of the teachers in advance and wring their hearts out with her pert little tummy. I knew the score! She'd tell the whole story over the phone, and I'm not deaf! The telephone had a short lead and you couldn't move it very far, you had to keep the door wedged halfway open. So I heard all the news. Anyway she was doing her exams and I meanwhile was sending encouraging letters anticipating an amnesty, summer, freedom to that terrible netherworld of human beings where my poor tormented Andrei was languishing. And my daughter meantime kept trying to feed up her Sasha. Inwardly I'd already got used to him and called him the infernal wretch, no doubt by rhymed association with paternal. Alyona had long since stopped writing to Andrei, and in my daily cheery letters I simply sent him her greetings and explained her silence on the grounds that she was doing her exams. I wrote that I was afraid Alyona was working too hard and worried that she'd end up in hospital – speak of the devil and he's bound to turn up (look what happened in the end).

That evening I dragged myself home from the library where I'd been gathering material for a newspaper column ('From the Courtroom' – you've got to make a living somehow), and of course it was impossible to work at home with all the noise and aggression I had to put up with – guffaws of laughter, slamming of doors, long sagas over the telephone featuring me in the principal role as the crazy mother, they were getting especially good mileage out of the story of the handyman with gonorrhoea, ha ha ha! – and when I got home I was greeted by total silence. No one home at ten at night. I had supper (hurrah!) in the empty kitchen, had a nice long bath in peace and comfort, calmly and happily climbed into my bed with the nice clean sheets, only to wake again at midnight as usual – but this time because of the complete silence all around. I got up and started pacing up and down in front of their door, then finally in panic knocked – not a sign of life. I glanced in – no one there. I went in – the covers had been thrown over the couch but there was a drop of dried blood on the bedspread. Rust-colour on the blue. My first thought was that he had killed her. And the second – immediately – that she had gone into labour.

Sasha came home at two in the morning thoroughly inebriated, infernal wretch, and staggered past me in silence to the lavatory, where the scoundrel promptly threw up.

'What's happened?' I asked him through the door. 'What's happened? Where's Alyona?'

He flushed the chain and emerged pale as putty.

'Given birth,' he said.

'Congratulations. To what?'

'A boy.'

'Where are they?'

'Maternity hospital 25' – and he collapsed like a drunken pig.

I left him lying where he'd fallen – I wasn't his mother to go dragging him off to bed – then I cleaned up after him in the lavatory and rushed into their room, found a bundle of old baby clothes and spent the whole night washing and boiling up the bits and pieces they'd managed to get hold of through friends. My bonny baby, however, came home from the maternity hospital all dressed in lace, because by that time I'd managed systematically to ring up every lady of my acquaintance, brightly inform them of the joyful event, and taking no notice of their evident bewilderment ask straight out whether by any chance not necessarily they, but perhaps someone they knew, might have anything they'd kept for a newborn baby (there's absolutely zilch in the shops, not a thing to be had, I lied smoothly – it wasn't true of course, there was the odd thing on sale but not, alas, for the likes of us). And I wasn't above asking if anyone had some old sheets too, soft ones that could be torn up for nappies. Following my enquiries the wretch was sent out like a hired hand to gather up the booty, he even came back with a block of baby soap – even I have to say did some ironing, falling into a trance and taking for ever over it; but come the evenings he'd vanish regular as clockwork and the same old story would ensue, culminating as usual with me cleaning the lavatory. I categorically forbade him to bring anyone home, telling him that a home with a baby in it was no place for riffraff of that kind, the whole place would be crawling with bugs in no time. That's what I told him. He heard what I had to say, every day he took Alyona some chicken in a jar, a thermos of broth and some juice, I emptied my purse for them – he didn't have a bean of course, that puppy. His father, the famous Timofei senior, had died at sea, they never recovered the body, his mother went everywhere looking for him, and since then it seems she'd spent her whole life going from one hospital to another, she's certified Class 2 Disabled. I asked what his mother's complaint was – what came to my mind straight away was tuberculosis, that would be the last straw if we all got infected – but it turned out to be schizophrenia. Thanks a lot! After this pleasant little conversation in the kitchen the wretch again vanished for the night. At this point Alyona rang up in a weak voice from the hospital, started telling me quite normally that the boy was beautiful with curly hair (I saw these famous curls when he came home, four little coils of hair stuck to his skull, otherwise he was as bald as Chairman Mao and with eyes in the same vein). Whereupon I answered that everyone in our family, men and women, had been beautiful when they were born, she and Andrei had also been the loveliest babies in the world, at which point I burst into tears. And she hastily said goodbye, having ascertained that the wretch wasn't at home and God knows where he was.

And now the paternal wretch and I were setting off impatiently in a twosome to see our Darling. The nurses picked him up and handed him to the wretch, I did the done thing and gave the sister three roubles, managed straight away to get hold of a rather grimy-looking taxi in which another mother-to-be, close on middle age, red-faced, had driven all alone to the hospital. Shapeless and doubled up, she should have been carried to the door, she was staggering along almost bent in two, clutching her solitary suitcase with her baby's layette, but I was slow on the uptake, so delighted to find a free taxi I just dashed blindly past the poor mother-to-be, narrowly missed knocking her over, and by way of thanks found the car seat awash with water. I informed the driver of this straight away, he climbed out morosely with his rag and silently started mopping down the interior of his battered old vehicle, casting an oath in the direction of the scrunched-up woman-in-labour whose baby's head had obviously reached the perineum by now, she was crawling along in a daze, bent double with that poor old suitcase. It keeps coming back to me now, I keep thinking of her and wishing we could meet again and I could offer my congratulations on the baby. At that moment she was all blotchy, just like a tortoise, barely heaving herself along the ground, but now I suppose assuming the child survived she'd be a fine handsome mum aged forty or thereabouts and the child would be six years old already – if indeed as I say it survived. Ah, mothers, mothers! It's the holiest of words, but time goes by and you'll find you have nothing to say to your child, and your child has nothing to say to you. Love them and they'll tear you to pieces, don't love them and they'll leave you all the same. That's how it is, aye, that's how it is, alas.

So I led my little trio to that (metaphorically) shat-upon car seat – it was nothing really, just plain old water. Holy water indeed, the water that had borne a child. The driver was a flabby, malicious-looking creature; he was obviously making a mental resolution to have nothing more to do with this female business and kept glancing suspiciously at my innocent little saint, convinced we were going to start flooding the car out again. The wretch was carrying his child in outstretched arms while She kept on fussing over his lacy bonnet. A fly was buzzing round the taxi, obviously attracted by the wet rag, there's no denying it's a bloody business, and it being springtime the fly was doubtless pregnant too. It's all part of the business we have to go through – dirt, blood, sweat, filth – and of course if you don't wash and clean up there are bound to be flies, His Majesty had been living like a lord in my home, spilling stuff all over the table, chucking the dishes in the sink without washing them. Still, after all that sweat and toil there he was, I had him before me, my darling, I saw him everywhere and in everything, I even came to recognise his wide brow in the face of the wretch, and his little mouth – three cherries. What can you say, I've no idea how the wretch came by his fine features, in any case he's gone for good now, gone for the big catch – marrying a foreigner, though judging by the alimony he doesn't earn all that much. My Alyona just served as a springboard for him, nothing more, she never gave him what for, as they say, just danced attendance on him day and night.

Sixteen days flashed by in a dream, night and day ceased to exist. I was on the go the whole time, forever washing, boiling, ironing, and my soggy mother hen of a daughter was suffering from constipation and cracked nipples plus inflammation of the mammary glands. Which meant a high fever, and Tima crying of course, and the wretch stalking around pale as death. I just kept my mouth shut. She, meanwhile, forbade me even to touch the child simply because I'd happened to mention that the wretch and some friend of his (while I was out at the library) had again eaten the entire contents of the fridge late one night, so that the following morning it was – oh my God! nothing in the house! and – oh my God! disaster! And I wasn't going to go bringing things home now – why chuck everything into the bottomless pit of Ternopol, I hadn't been hired to

52

serve his needs on top of everything else, that's what I told her, going into their little lair where it was warm and smelled of milk and fresh linen from the clean nappies I'd brought in from the balcony. The sweet smell of the nursery, where my little sunshine was sleeping away with his bulging brow and the fluffy dark down on his little head. My joy. But I was torn to pieces – Andrei was coming home and how was I going to feed him? Where was he going to live? What on earth was going to happen? I couldn't sleep a wink, I'd fall asleep and wake again, fall asleep and wake and lie there drenched in sweat. And meanwhile we had this extra weight hung round our necks, there the whole time, supposedly working for his exams. Have mercy on us, daughter, can't you get rid of him? We'd be much better off without him, I'll help you out, what do we need him for? What, I ask you? Just so he can gobble up everything you've got? Just so you can dance on all fours before him begging his pardon every five minutes? But all I actually said was:

'Why doesn't that wretch of yours go and get himself some work, go off to the taiga or somewhere. Go and do some good hard labour like his dad. You can't sleep with him now in any case! And I'm not prepared to feed him any longer.'

Dry-eyed, she replied:

'Not a hope. He's my husband. Why don't you just leave us alone and go scribble your stupid poems!'

'Stupid, okay. No doubt some of them are. But that's how I feed the lot of you!' I replied, unperturbed.

Sooner or later we always got round to the subject

of my poems, the scribbles she was so ashamed of. As for me, if I didn't write I'd simply curl up and die, my heart would break. But what I said was:

'In other words, let him go off and start earning his living. Andrei's coming home any day now. They've declared an amnesty.'

As a matter of fact I'd actually overheard the wretch trying to fix up some job or other to do with concrete, heard his heated mutterings over the phone, saying he could do this that and the other and claiming all sorts of qualifications.

'Don't go counting your chickens,' says she. 'Declarations don't mean a thing.'

'I see, so that's what you're hoping, is it? That's what you're hoping – Andrei won't be released at all? Well, I assure you he will be. I found out, I went to see a lawyer. And I don't want Andrei with his nervous disposition going to pieces all over again, this time just because of that wretch of yours. He's going to be the end of him, I know it,' I said loudly, counting on the wretch overhearing in our little apartment. Tima started squealing in his bed and she threw himself at him with exaggerated concern, and it then turned out the wretch was standing right there behind me keeping his mouth shut as usual. Anyway what could he say, what could anyone say that was new round here? Everything hung like a sword in the air, our whole life was on the point of collapse. The trap was about to slam shut, as it was every day, but now into the bargain some huge great log was crashing down on top of us. In the ensuing silence everyone crawled away looking beaten up; only Tima went on squealing pitifully, lamenting his hunger, his mother's exhaustion, his wretched father's silence and indifference, my poverty, my son Andrei's long days in prison camp.

Yet the days went by and Andrei did come home. And the wretch, as I've related already, locked himself in the lavatory (or attempted to) and I said to Andrei:

'I beg you, be quiet, listen. I didn't write because what was the point of writing that Alyona was walking round with a great fat belly fetched from God knows where? It would only have worried you.'

'Alyona?'

'Yes. God knows who the wretch was.'

'Hold on, what about him?'

'That was later – listen and I'll tell you properly.'

'I'm hungry, my head's spinning, Ma, that's enough.'

'Just a minute, I'll give you your soup. You haven't yet heard the main thing. Have some bread. Have you washed your hands?'

No answer, as usual. It's always been a problem, this business of washing hands. He looked at me in that odd ambiguous way of his, took the bread in his dirty hands and broke it.

'All right, you're a grown-up boy, do as you please. So anyway, I took steps.'

'You did?'

'On Alyona's behalf. I did, of course, who else but me?'

'You didn't take many on my behalf.'

Jealous as always!

'Andrei darling, there are lots of things I did you never got to hear about in there.'

'All I know is that one person did time on behalf of eight.'

'Shut up and listen. You alone got punished, so it was one against five, wasn't it?'

'I've heard all this before. It's crap.'

'Don't talk nonsense. Listen. That was why you got just two years. If it'd been eight – in fact thirteen altogether – against just one, and him getting trampled to pieces, can you imagine? So that's enough of that! I went and saw him in hospital.'

'I got the standard sentence.'

'Don't be ridiculous!'

'Huh.'

'If the whole eight of you had turned up in court, every one of you would have got at least five years. Now d'you understand?'

'Shu-u-ut up! Bitch!'

'Andrei, son, I beg you, calm down!' I said. 'You're home again, my sunshine! Light of my whole life! And you're going to defend me against that wretch!'

The wretch meanwhile was stuck in the lavatory desperately rattling the bolt; he couldn't get it open now.

'So now let me tell you properly. You eat up. I'd like you to know I did indeed take steps, the girls in her group all came forward to testify about what had gone on in the hayloft and how she tried to wash the blood out of her slip back in September.'

'Shut up, Ma, you're making me dizzy.'

'And because of those girls he was made to sign on the dotted line. Eat up now, there's potatoes, look, and herring – he didn't quite manage to eat the lot. Wretch!'

I couldn't even cry.

'The things we've been through! And it turns out he's more or less an orphan. From darkest Ternopol. He only just scraped a place at the institute and there they were threatening to throw him in the army.'

'If it'd been me I'd have gone. Rather the army any day.'

'Well the wretch didn't go.'

'A nice young man you've gone and dragged home. Ma, you're a bitch.'

'Eat up, now, eat up, it's all good home cooking.'

At this point in comes the Ternopol orphan, hands freshly washed, cocks open his mouth and utters these strange words:

'Pleased to meet you.'

'Andrei.'

'Sasha.'

The wretch was the first to hold out his hand. Sometimes a streak of sense slips into him.

Then Alyona rushes in all unbuttoned (she was still feeding), eagerly bursts into sobs and flings herself at Andrei.

'Silly thing, she's always been like that,' Andrei said cordially.

'What can you do?' the wretch agreed. I could have scratched his eyes out.

Oddly enough, Alyona and the two young men

looked very good against the background of our poor dirty kitchen. The light of youth, the light of hope still burned in their eyes – ah, if they'd only known or guessed what awaited them then, apart from this darkness and the only thing that can ever warm your heart amid the dark – the soft breathing of a little child, our darling.

I love him passionately, physically. The pleasure of holding in my hand his own tiny weightless one, of looking into those round, dark blue eyes with lashes so long – as my favourite author wrote – the shadow of them falls on his cheeks. And on everything else nearby – you can even see their shadow on the wall when he sits up in bed in the lamplight. Great thick curling lashes, little fans! All parents, and grand-parents especially, love their babies physically like this, make them make up for everything else in life. It's sinful love, I tell you, it makes the child callous and unbridled, as if it understands there's some-thing unclean in it all. But what can you do? Nature intended us to love. Once love was let loose it stretched its wings to cover everyone, even those it was never meant for – the old. Poor old souls, you warm your old hearts too!

So they stood there in the kitchen, my two loved ones, my children, and I was neither here nor there, redundant.

'So,' I said.

Neither of them stirred.

'I object to having that man registered here, Andrei. And she in turn objects to your being registered on the grounds you're just back from camp. That's what she's threatening to do, anyway, she says she has the right.'

Oh, the power of words!

'What do you mean?' Andrei asked.

'I'll tell you all about it later,' Alyona said wearily. 'Come and look at our little fellow now.'

'How could you?' he asked, bewildered.

'Come on now, it was only my way of getting back at her. You know it's the law of the jungle in here.'

'All right, all right.'

The pair of them, Alyona and the wretch, went off into their room like a couple of drooping flowers. Andrei sat down to eat. I sat down opposite.

'Andrei!'

'Ma!'

'Just give me two minutes. Andrei, we really are in deep trouble here. She wants to have him registered, she fails to see what the wretch is up to. He's just using her as a springboard. He'll take her to court and wangle the room from her! That's where it's heading!'

'He's a good-looking guy. Really.' He gave an odd laugh.

'Yes, he could have had his pick. If it hadn't been for my witnesses. But as the saying goes, he's bent on snatching his tuft from a mangy sheep. He'll up and leave as soon as he's got his registration.'

I said all this unashamedly out loud. And I was right! It turned out I was right one hundred per cent, but how to prove it? It took every ounce of my strength to prove the truth! Because the wretch got quite attached to his Tima. He fell in love with him, just as I said, physically, gave him his bath, was so proud of him, the little shrimp, took him for walks and showed him off to all the greedy guests who came for their free meals. He loved him! It was all so complicated . . .

Suddenly no one needed me at all.

'Can't you see?' I said to Alyona, stopping her in the hall. 'Your husband has homosexual tendencies. He's in love with the boy.'

Alyona gave me a crazed look.

'It isn't you he loves.' I spelled it out. 'It's him. It's unnatural.'

Alyona opened her mouth and guffawed. It was true she'd just been weeping in her room, as was evident even in the darkness of the hall. The wretch still wasn't home at eleven o'clock at night.

'Darling child!' I wanted to give her a hug but Alyona, laughing with odd relief, went and took the telephone and secreted herself in her room, half-shutting the door. The endless theme of these telephone conversations, of course, was me; she could go on about me till the cows came home.

And how old was I at the time? No more than fifty!

Alyona was nineteen and Andrei twenty.

It seems so long ago now that they were born, the two of them just a year apart. The result of a fit of madness on an archaeological dig and of my getting someone wrong, as usual, on a magnificent scale. I was just a young thing of twenty-nine at the time with a haircut like a boy's, skinny as anything, all eyes and long legs, still just a girl (right at the beginning before any of us had got to know each other I was standing with one of the boys behind a rock looking at some rusty fragment he'd found, and suddenly *he* came up to us, it was so funny, and said: 'What are you boys doing here?' I raised my eyes to him, he looked again and choked – I was so like a boy at the time. That was how it all began, days and nights of happiness, when I was just a young poetess, fresh from teachers' training, chucked out of a newspaper where I'd been a temporary trainee for having an affair with a married artist, the father of three chil-dren whom I was seriously proposing to bring up myself, little fool that I was! And his wife turns up and says: aren't you ashamed of yourself? – and goes straight to the editor-in-chief. There and then they were given the three-room apartment they'd been promised for years – they'd been living all this time in one single room, the whole lot of them including his mother-in-law – and in my room he'd found the peace and quiet to work, though my mother in turn was forever hurling accusations at him for being a millstone round my neck and not doing the proper thing – how long have we all been singing these same old songs!) Anyway there I was, sacked from the paper and off on a whim on an archaeological dig, and they were the eventual result of it all, Andrei and Alyona, my two rays of sunshine, and once again it was everybody living in one room, my mother stubbornly shutting herself up in hers! So time went by and we had our taste of real life and he went ahead with his divorce, divorce on the grand scale in the town of Kuibyshev; his wife turned up one day to inspect me and my big belly, or rather he opened the door one day and there they stood, his wife and their fifteen-year-old son – I've got to talk to you she says. They came in, she slapped me in the face, broke the window and slashed her wrist with one of the pieces, she was all covered in blood, he caught hold of her, the son was all pale and kept shouting: don't you dare touch Mum! Then my mother sticks her nose in, sees what's going on, brings in a bandage (she's so mean she went and got a used one, a bandage she'd had on her leg and washed out for further use, she loves bandaging herself up). Then she took them into her room and gave them a cup of tea, and we locked ourselves up in our room like two doves, beak to beak, and it was a good thing really his old wife burst in on the scene right then, everything had been turning sour already, he'd been getting all broody, missing his son and home, and archaeology wasn't much of a job, the pay was pretty mean, and then there was my big belly of course, and the alimony. He'd grown all pinched and worried. Then suddenly she bursts in and turns everything upside down – clever lady, a woman with a thirst for destruction can accomplish a great deal! She'll smash herself to pieces and then look what happens – it all starts afresh, some new destructive impulse gets going – and once again she'll have to pick up the pieces and start all over from scratch, that's how it goes – at least that's what happens to me, that's just how I am, just how I am with others.

*

So that's how it was, and not so long ago either. You look back on your life and the men run like milestones through it. Jobs and men, with children for chronology, just like in Chekhov. It all looks so vulgar and banal, but then what doesn't look banal from the outside. Alyona, I know, finds every little thing I say repulsive. For example, my asking some simple question like 'Is he interesting?' when she went blabbing on – this was years ago now, when she was in eighth grade – about her friend Lena and her love affairs. Just those simple words – is he interesting? – seemed utterly to dumbfound her, she'd go into a white rage, though all I meant was that her Lena was a filly who needed a good thrashing, I couldn't imagine anyone taking it into his head to make love to her, a real sledgehammer of a girl, at the age of fourteen she reeked like a navvy, size 7 feet, the hair on her head all black and bristly like a shoebrush, a few young whiskers sprouting on her chin and a couple of poles sticking out like props underneath her huge rump. My Alyona (all the girls were Alyona or Lena that year, just as they're all Katyas now) worshipped this bewhiskered Lena of hers, it was forever Lena this and Lena that, and notwithstanding the state of relations between us, which had pretty well formed by the time she was fourteen (piss off, sod off, jump in the lake – or her favourite rejoinder, you're off your rocker Ma) – despite all this she'd be off at the drop of a hat with her rapturous legends of Lena – until, that is, I managed to get in a question:

'Is he interesting?'

'What's that supposed to mean?'

'Well, he must be rather an interesting fellow?'

'How come?'

When all I actually meant to say was this:

'I can't see anyone normal hankering after that hippopotamus Lena.'

'Ha ha ha! When it's me no one so much as looks at . . . '

It's a well-known fact that girls brought up without a father are saddled their whole lives with the rejected-wife complex and all its consequences.

'It's me no one'll look at. When Lena went on holiday to the Caucasus last year all the locals were after her. They thought she was eighteen years old! When she was only thirteen!'

'She was lucky they didn't take her for thirty.'

'Mu-um!' (Virtually shrieking by now.)

'Now listen to me: in the Caucasus anything goes, your granny's friend Aunty Olya was down there on holiday with her sister, both of them at the age of sixty-five were down on the beach in just their beach robes, bless them, and bare feet, and they were women of some size, I can tell you, they got their beach robes in Moscow and showed them to me, size 20 they were, and huge bras, 42 E, not that you could tell with them folded into those great bellies of theirs, poor dears, looking as if they'd give birth at any moment.'

'Give over, will you.'

'You listen to me now. Aunty Olya came back and told us: You'd never believe it, Sima dear, she says – to your granny this was – you'd never believe the success we had on the beach at Gagry, we had the old man with us, of course, my sister's husband, but he got fed up and wouldn't come out with us any more. We were just surrounded by them, they couldn't stop smacking their lips at us, even passers-by blew us kisses, there was no escaping them!'

'Mum, you're so . . .' she hisses, '. . . you're so . . . you're just disgusting.'

'So tell me now, this fellow of Lena's an interesting type, I suppose? From the Caucasus too, is he?'

'Why d'you have to keep on at me?' (She's almost weeping now.)

But the point was – I saw it all so clearly – this Lena wasn't worth my Alyona's little finger. My little daughter, my beauty Alyona, my quiet little nestling who was such a comfort to me after all the adolescent storms with Andrei – the things she would say to me when she was only nine years old! Such wise comforting words when I split up with their father, and their grandmother, of course, was the final straw! That summer he'd found someone else on yet another of these expeditions, it was the same scenario over again, only on this occasion he had his son and daughter with him, and when he came back Alyona said to me:

'They loved us all so much there, Mummy, you should have seen it when we were having our farewell campfire – that lady Lera just cried and cried! Cried and cried!'


So a month later after various long-distance phone calls, his face all covered in boils out of nerves, my husband left for good, this time to Krasnodar where he's living to this day with the weeping Lera, some son or other of hers and the woman's blind mother; the children used to go and join him on various other digs until it became quite clear that he had no time for them. Lera had a one-room apartment and there was no prospect of her having my children to stay there. And then their daddy started going off God knows where – Rwanda or Burundi or wherever. No doubt it's a good way of strengthening international relations, but Africa means AIDS and there's good reason not to be over-optimistic for him on that score.

My mother, of course, always regarded their father as a sponger, dodger and the rest of it. What a melancholy triumph for her when he came to fetch his things and take his leave! What a demonstration she made! So sweet and tender all of a sudden with me, the cobra – she who lies weeping into her pillow now, forever complaining that everyone's stealing from her . . . when she always spoons the whole lot down in one gulp, so greedily, greedily – it's her diabetes.


So the alimony would arrive, forty roubles and not a kopeck more, but I was earning a bit too, I had a job answering letters in the poetry section of a journal. A man called Burkin had taken me under his wing – nice man, wispy beard and moustache, with trembling hands and such puffy cheeks he looked as if he had mumps on both sides. 'I'm stuck with it,' he'd say when I told him sympathetically that I couldn't stand dentists and their drills either, but if he had swollen gums on both sides he really should go, otherwise you never knew . . . I got one rouble per letter and sometimes there were up to sixty letters per month. And then I got a couple of poems published that year, both on International Women's Day, the fee was 18 roubles for the pair of them.

But what did nine-year-old Alyona have to say, wise little girl, when the door closed for the last time on their father and I stood there with a fixed grin, tearless, with burning cheeks, about to throw myself out the window so I would meet him there, for the last time, a shapeless carcass on the pavement. To punish him.

'Mum,' Alyona said, 'do I love you?'

'Yes,' I replied.


My beautiful daughter, how I adored her once, a baby in swaddling clothes, whose every finger washed, fondled, kissed a hundred times. How touching her little curls were (where are they now?), her huge shining eyes, bright as forget-me-nots, radiating goodness, innocence, tenderness – and all for me . . . Oh the days of their childhood! What bliss it was to love them, my two little nestlings, to see their sweet little heads on the pillows when they slept, there in my room so warm and quiet . . . 'Hair like a white flame . . . glimmers on the white pillow . . . little eyes and ears hidden . . . only the nose, at work, breathes in and out.' All gone to the dogs, alas! – squandered and stolen, flung at the feet of the first thing that came along: Lena. Not a day spent without her, not a thought devoted to anyone but her – Lena's whims drove the whole family mad. Andrei used to fight

with Alyona over the telephone, he'd be wanting
to call someone while she was eternally awaiting a
ring from that harpy – where would they go today,
whose birthday party was it, were they invited? The
pair of them, Andrei and Alyona, fought like mad
over everything. Alyona was forever shrieking and
coming running to me in the kitchen, mouth agape,
sobbing her eyes out and gasping for breath, *aaaah!*
Another pretty detail of our life together. At night
time, only at night time, I felt again the happiness of
motherhood. I'd cover them up, tuck them in, kneel
down by their beds . . . They didn't need my love. Or
rather, they would nave perished without me, yet I was
a nuisance to them. What a padarox! – as Nyura says,
our neighbour the bone-crusher.

Andrei played soccer and hockey; by the time he
was in ninth grade his head and face were all covered in scars like a tomcat's. The other kids all pale
with fright would bring him in from the yard; he'd
hobble in all covered in blood or with his foot
smashed in, or they'd carry him in unconscious (our
local activists in the block, encouraged by the new
political freedoms, had dug up the lawns, the bas-
tards, planted this and that and fixed an invisible
wire all round to guard their plantations, just at the
right level to catch a child's throat). Another time
the children were playing daggers with a broken bed
leg, steel of course. One fat kid, Vasya by name,
slipped and drove the thing into Andrei's leg. Once
– I was still young at the time, though it was after the
Krasnodar business – a friend of mine came to visit,
an interesting man, married and a serious drinker
(which didn't stop him being interesting).

'So, old man,' this friend said to Andrei when he'd been brought home yet again limping and leaving a bloody trail in the lift (later I cleaned it up and had a good weep), 'what is it this time, a fragmentation wound?'

'M'm,' said Andrei.

One evening six years later Andrei didn't come home at all; he arrived back eventually at two in the morning. Granny met him in the hall and was beside herself. 'Get back where you've come from!' she yelled and hurled a stool at him, and something just snapped in my heart. In the morning I phoned up this same friend, Arkady Yakovlevich, and in a cheerful voice – he always sounded cheerful just after a big drinking spree and before he'd got going on the next – he said:

'Anna Andrianovna, you ought to call emergencies just in case, even though women don't often get heart attacks' (from which it was clear that Arkady Yakovlevich had been in a men's cardiological ward but had failed to glance into the women's one).

Then he asked what was up. And then he asked how old Andrei was.

'Do you really want him to jump up from a woman's bed crying "Mummy's expecting me home at ten"? I got a girl pregnant when I was just fifteen, and he's sixteen already.'

He was always so reassuring, Arkady Yakovlevich. We'd met through work, I'd been doing a job for Masha putting together an anthology of poetry on the theme of labour, I'd already been dropped by the publishing house and everywhere else – it's a long story – and couldn't even show my face there, and it was supposed to be Masha who was editing the book, later she gave me twenty-five per cent and a couple of tenners in payment. I was glad even of that. To cut a long story short, A.Y. was the son of a poet who wrote precisely on the theme of labour; I'd come across his father's verse while working in the library, I'd happened to glance at a collection of his and saw he had two poems in honour of the October Revolution and two in honour of May Day, all four on the theme of labour. I go to a bit of trouble over these things, so I rang this Yakov Dobrynin up. A man answered and told me he wasn't there, I asked when he'd be home, to which this male voice replied that there was unfortunately no answer to that question. I was a bit taken aback, but I went ahead and explained what the problem was and that was how I got to know Arkady, truly a very nice man, whose wife however assumed my visits could mean only one thing – that's what they tend to assume, the wives, though they're always perfectly polite; in one case the wife of a poet I'd arranged to drop in on late one evening to collect some poems of mine – I'd asked him to take a look at the manuscript and tell me frankly whether it was worth my carrying on – this wife of his when I rang the bell that evening came out to meet me in her birthday suit, just hugging her breasts together to cover them. As if to say 'We're already in bed.' Befriending the wives (to adapt Pushkin's words) is never the easiest of things.

*

70

Night.

But let me start from the beginning. My shrill little darling's already asleep, little arms and legs spread out, orphan that you are, poor darling, now Grandma can be alone at last with paper and pencil, I can't afford a pen, Andrei has robbed me seriously this time, not just like the last time when he stood there raging on the stairs and as a farewell gesture set fire to my letter box, demanding I hand over twenty-five roubles, no more no less, uttering into the bargain the foulest oaths and meanwhile systematically hammering on the door with his heels – while I and the kid (I covered his ears) huddled together in the kitchen.

'I'm moving in,' yells Andrei, 'and you'd better (unprintable) hand it over, you so-and-so, give me the twenty-five! You've taken my room (unprintable) so pay up now, (unprintable) Mother!'

'Mother' in the foulest of mother curses.

My little star didn't cry, he just trembled. But luckily Andrei himself is a coward. I clutched Tima to me, but in the end I couldn't restrain myself and yelled at him threateningly:

'That's enough now! I'm calling the police! That's enough!'

Andrei's incapable of believing I would ever call the police – for whom? For him, unhappy boy, who's never as it is got over his time in camp, can't forget what they did to him there, never recovered as a person but kept hanging round with his so-called friends – on whose behalf he'd been locked up in the first place – kept reproaching them and blackmailing them for a tenner or a fiver – or so I

71

reckon, because once the crazy mother of one of his fellow-defendants was trying to track him down; the phone rang and this loathsome voice came on the line:

'Hello! Hello!'

'Hello,' I said.

'Hello!' (Shouting hysterically.) 'Can I . . . is that the So-and-Sos' house? Hello!'

'No,' I replied.

'Isn't Andrei So-and-So there? Hello!' (Hysterical.)

'He doesn't live here. Who are you?'

'Never you mind.'

Weli, goodbye in that case. But she wouldn't let me go.

'Hello! Hello! Where is he?'

'I've no idea.'

'Isn't he working at the fire station any more? I rang there.'

What a bitch!

'No, he's at the ministry now.'

Let her go ringing every single department of every single ministry.

'Oh yes? Can you give me his number? Hello!'

You could just see her, panic-stricken, ears aflame.

'It's ex-directory,' I said.

'F . . . '

'I don't know who you're talking about.'

'It's his friend Ivan's mother speaking. He came to visit' when I wasn't there and walked off with a leather jacket. Hello! Can you hear me?'

'Go and look for it at your son's then. What's happened to him, anyway, hasn't he been jailed yet over

the Alyosha K. affair? The case is going for a new
hearing!'

(It was her son who'd been wearing Andrei's
sweater to this day; it had cost me my last rouble, I'd
bought it for Andrei's birthday.)

'Incidentally,' I said, 'could Ivan refund me the
value of the things he's stolen from me?'

She slams down the phone.


A terrible dark force / a mad blind passion / to fall
at the feet of my beloved son / like the prodigal son
himself! (my verse).

Andrei came back from camp and ate my herring,
my potatoes, my black bread, drank my tea and
devoured my mind as always and sucked my blood,
he was flesh of my flesh but yellow, filthy, tired to
death. I said nothing. The words 'Go and take a
shower' stuck in my throat like an insult that
wouldn't come out. Ever since childhood he'd been
outraged to the point of nausea by those few words
(no doubt he felt humiliated by them, reminded of
just what he was worth, all sweaty and dirty, alongside me, always spotlessly clean, twice a day in the
shower for a good long session: oh the warmth of
something other! The warmth of good hot Soviet
water, for lack of anything better!).

'Give me some money.'

'What money?' I cried. 'Whose money? I'm working for three as it is!'

Yes! And I'm a fourth! Everyone here is out to
suck me dry!

So I stood there shouting with just five roubles in

my purse and the bit in my savings bank, Mother's insurance, plus the bit I'd stashed away behind the skirting board for a rainy day when I'd been given the five translations done from a crib from languages I didn't know a word of, that was after telling every stranger and acquaintance I ran into that my dissident son was in prison on a false charge and my daughter to all intents a single mother and I had two students without a grant on my hands and now a grandson into the bargain and oh dear, the nappies and the booties.

'You know what, you could do with a wash . . . shall I run you a bath?'

He stared at my collarbone and slowly blinked.

'I bought you some jeans, you know, Soviet-made – don't laugh – and some summer shoes – why don't you go and get changed, and have a nice shower first.'

'I don't want to get changed. I'm okay like this. Give me the money, I need it.'

'How much is it exactly you need?'

'Fifty to go on with.'

'Hah! I've got five roubles for tomorrow's food, and that's it. *He* eats everything, I've been literally hiding the food in my room. Shall I give you three?'

'Fifty's what I need. If that's the way it is I'll have to go kill someone.'

'Kill me.'

'Andrei.'

My beautiful daughter was standing in the doorway.

'Come and get it from us, Andrei, Sasha got his grant yesterday, we'll give it to you, she'd be hanged sooner than give hers away.'

74

So Andrei sloped off with those fifty roubles in his pocket and didn't return for two days, and in the meantime the police came round asking where's A. and said he wouldn't be allowed to register. A great panic ensued, and Alyona and I applied on the spot to get both of them registered, Andrei and Sasha. Brushed off our differences, so to speak, and came to a deal, like countries exchanging spies. My first concern was that Andrei might really have gone and done something mad.

But two days later he came home all newly kitted out in a jeans suit with a shoulder bag, properly shaved and accompanied by a couple of tarts of such extraordinary appearance I thought my heart would give out. Alyona came out for a moment then disappeared, retreated into her warm nappy-filled abode. He took the two sluts into my room and spent exactly an hour there, although I kept quietly knocking on the door, delicately rapping with my nails to tell him I needed my things, my precious money was sitting right there behind the skirting board. Alyona, walking past, just kicked that accursed locked door with her heel.

When they unlocked it I said, holding out my hand:
'Fifty roubles.'
'. . . !'
'I gave Alyona back what you took.'

The tarts were standing there in the doorway and he was digging round in my cupboard, going through all my things.

'What are you doing? I've packed up all your stuff, the suitcase is up there look . . . '

Oh the bleeding hearts of a mother and son, how

powerful and dangerous they are! Where are you, dear little boy who smelt of phlox and meadows of camomile?

'The local police came round and warned . . . '

'To hell with them . . . '

'You wouldn't be registered . . . '

Oh bleeding hearts!

'Oh yeah?'

'We'll have you registered, Andrei, don't get upset, don't worry.'

'I'm not worrying. I'm getting married, and your registration can get stuffed.'

'Who on earth are you getting married to, them?'

'And what's wrong with them?'

The two sluts burst into shrill laughter, giving us a good view of their bad teeth.

'By the way, where's Granny?'

'I didn't want to write . . . Granny's taken a turn for the worse.'

'What, kicked the bucket has she?'

'Worse than that. The worst that can happen to anyone. You understand? Do you understand?'

'But where is she?'

'In mental hospital, where else could she be?'

'Stuffed her in the bin, have you?'

He took his suitcase and they all trooped off.

Night. Silence. Downstairs my neighbour Nyura is gouging out bones. Tomorrow she'll make them into soup.

The odd thing is that Miriam Abramovna, the doctor in charge at the psychiatric hospital, is such a calm, self-assured, even reassuring person. In one of our conversations she said something very relevant to the above and true in general: out there, she said, beyond the confines of the hospital, there are many more madmen than there are here inside; for the most part, she said, the patients in the hospital are quite normal people who just lack for something, she didn't say what. Well I've got a few things lacking too, I couldn't help thinking then, I realise now I behaved like a complete fool when it finally came to a head: in the first conversations I had with her I couldn't stop crying and complaining how Mother had very nearly set fire to the whole apartment, how she'd filled the whole place with gas and so on, we'd left her alone for two weeks in the summer and when we returned we'd found the whole balcony full of worms and flocks of birds sitting there and these huge fat flies crawling all over the place and it turned out she'd bought some meat and then gone and forgotten that she'd left it outside on the balcony. The stench of it! Altogether that was a terrible period, Andrei kept getting summonses and being dragged off to the police station, I once went with him and the investigator shouted at me. Andrei would return home yellow and lifeless and the others kept on ringing up and bullying him, he would just nod and say nothing, and the parents of those blasted friends of his in inverted commas kept demanding to see him, dragging him off and obviously talking him into taking the entire blame on himself, and Mother couldn't understand what was going on at all and kept repeating anxiously that the boy wasn't himself and wasn't eating anything, and

77

the girl had come home late yesterday and there was green all over the back of her light raincoat, obviously she'd been lying flat on her back somewhere; and then suddenly Mother had gone all quiet, shut herself in her room and virtually stopped coming out, this coinciding with the time Andrei left early one morning to go for questioning and then never came back. She didn't even ask where he was. The months went by and she kept carefully laying out her teeth on the sideboard, they'd fallen out of their own accord, and one day she triumphantly presented me with a packet full of bloody cotton wool just to show me, she said, what a haemorrhage she'd had from her throat! Why did she do it? What's all this about, I asked her, what commission d'you suppose you're presenting evidence to, let me throw it away. And what's this you're wearing, Mother? What's happened to you? You've got a whole wardrobe full of clothes, I'm the one who has nothing to wear, but you? It suddenly dawned on me then that she was saving up all her good things for better times, as if she actually believed that one fine day the crowds would part and out she'd step in her new autumn coat or her fine wool dress and then (attention everyone!) someone would up and propose to her. She even joked that we had to take good care of her for her fiancé, to which I replied 'Who's he, a pensioner? D'you want to spend the rest of your life trailing after a pensioner?', not daring even to go into it and find out what sort of fiancé she really had in mind. She looked at me with her little eyes, grey once but now reduced to a speck of blue, all the colour in her had faded, neutralised – the eyes a dim, childish blue the colour of moonlight. Beaming at me, she replied that she couldn't stand pensioners and wasn't planning to spend her life carting chamber pots around. The question remained who exactly she was saving herself for, and alas the only answer that presented itself was that she still awaited and sincerely believed in the return of youth. Somewhere in the depths of her consciousness she still counted on better times, awaited the moment when she would suddenly come to, shake off this outer shell and burst into bloom again, just as she'd bloom afresh once upon a time after going on holiday. In the depths of her soul, in other words, she was waiting for – what? Heavenly paradise? – But instead what happened was this: one day she called me quietly to her room and explained that 'they'd come for her'.

'And why should they do that?'

'Shhh!'

'Who on earth are you talking about, for heaven's sake?'

'Look' – she twisted her head as far as she could away from me and the window – 'over there.'

'Where, what is all this nonsense?'

'Look down below.'

I looked down and saw that it was raining.

'I can't see anything. There's nothing there.'

'They're coming again.'

'Who?!'

'It starts with "A".'

'What does, what are you on about?'

'Shhh, don't shout,' she whispered, 'the ambulance.'

I looked again. Sure enough an ambulance was heading down the street.

'So what?'

'I went out of the house yesterday as soon as . . . you know . . . and they were after me straight away. A policeman started following me, I turned round on purpose and started walking towards him. Walked up to him on purpose and laughed in his face. I'm not afraid of them!'

Well, well, well . . . I stood numbly in the kitchen, then went into Alyona's room and told her her grandmother had gone mad, to which she replied that it was I who was mad. I countered by saying that it was nothing terrible, such things do happen – indeed that was how my aunt had finished up, though she went on living a long time afterwards. It was hereditary. Alyona abruptly got up and went in to see her grandmother. I heard them talking quietly, then Alyona started weeping and saying 'How awful'. I told her that she should have listened to me a long time ago and gone to see a psychiatrist herself. Alyona, as always, burst out laughing, not knowing that I'd already gone to see a psychiatrist and had got her registered as a psychiatric out-patient; in fact a therapist had already been to see her in the guise of an ordinary doctor, though Alyona as if to order had answered all his questions extremely rudely and sharply, and when he asked 'Why aren't you at the institute, what are you doing just lolling about on an unmade bed?', she'd jumped up and demonstratively rushed off to the lavatory where, for a good five minutes, she kept pulling the chain until the doctor finally upped and left.

'Do you consider yourself normal?' I threw in as an afterthought. 'Take a look at yourself. You've missed classes again, you're up the whole night reading and then you can't get up in the morning. Classic psychosis. That's what heredity does. That's what it does, darling girl.'

The only reason I did it was to shake her out of herself, give her a bit of a shock; my heart was bleeding – my mother mad, my son in prison, pray for me, pray for me (as *she* wrote, our great genius). I wanted to reawaken my daughter's mind, rouse her from the sleep of reason, the torpor she'd slipped into as a result of Andrei's imprisonment, her bad marks at college, her acne, her so-called first love – she kept a diary about it all which I read.

*No one must read this diary or I'll leave for good. Neither Mum nor Granny nor Andrei! No one! Yesterday there was a seminar at Dr Tamarskaya's. S. came and sat right in front of me and kept on turning round and giving me strange dreamy looks, head bowed and laughing to himself all the while. Lena was carrying on with him and telling jokes and I just sat there sober as anything, pretending I couldn't care less when my heart was in my boots. After the lecture Lena and I left, and suddenly in the cloakroom she said to me: 'S. wants to spend New Year's Eve with you! He told me.' I just shrugged my shoulders, no one could have guessed how my heart was thumping with triumph! I could barely walk! S. and I together on New Year's Eve!*

**22 December**. *Lena told me again that S. must be in love with me, he keeps on asking about me. If anyone asks if he's going to the movies he always wants to know if*

*Alyona's going to be there, and then doesn't go since I'm not. While she was telling me all this Lena kept looking testingly at me. She wants confirmation. I know of course that she's in love with him, but she'd never guess my feelings . . . I couldn't sleep at all last night from happiness. In the morning I dreamt about S., dreamt he and I were driving in an open convertible and I was somehow enveloped by his warmth. Today he was nowhere to be seen. I have to exercise my strength of will! I should do gymnastics every morning. Last time I saw him S. said he'd got up at midday.*

**30 December**. *Tomorrow is New Year's Eve. I barely struggled through my exam. I cried in Room Seven. Lena went all quiet and wouldn't say anything. S. was first in for the exam and left straight away. I was late as usual. I asked her, 'So, where are you and S. going to spend New Year's?' It took all my courage and I sounded so malevolent. She answered as if nothing had happened: S. and I are going to the party at the Transport Institute Club. I didn't tell you, S. said he didn't want to go anywhere with anyone on New Year's Eve, he would just sleep through it at home, he can't stand these holidays. And Lena had bought them both tickets to the Transport Institute party, there was going to be champagne and presents and a disco, American movies and a fancy dress ball. I asked as a matter of interest what films they were going to show, and she just answered 'American' and said the tickets were sold out already, supposedly she'd tried to get hold of some money to buy me a ticket as well but there were none left. The tickets were quite expensive. If you like, she said, we'll all go together and try to get hold of a spare ticket at ten o'clock? I said forget it. She said we could think up a costume for me, she was going to go as a witch and tell*

82

*everyone's fortune with cards and she was going to dress up
S. in her father's silk shirt with a hankie knotted at one side
and a patch over his eye like a pirate. After which I turned
tail and went home like a beaten dog. Granny was telling
Mum off for not bringing me up properly, she spends the
whole night reading, Granny was saying, and look at the
result, she can't even get up when she's got her exams. If
only they'd lay off me and take a look at their darling
Andrei for a change, he even smokes for Christ's sake!*

*1 January. Sensation. Lena and S. weren't at the
Transport do! I went there at 10 o'clock feeling a complete
fool wearing Granny's black dress with a rose in my hair
(Carmen with her fan, Granny gave it to me and dressed
me up), bought an ordinary ticket with no problem at all
and went in to find the hall half-empty and freezing cold
with dreadful blaring music, all howls and yells, and people doing some kind of ballroom dancing. When it was
almost midnight I joined the queue – luckily not too long –
for a glass of champagne, you could buy a little packet with
a present in it too if you wanted. I gulped down the champagne when the hands moved on the big clock in the hall
and went home to bed without waiting for the disco. Mum
and Granny were having their annual row, sitting in front
of the telly all red in the face and shouting. As usual it was
about Andrei, who hasn't shown up for three days now, he
rang up and Granny rushed to answer, but Mum grabbed
the phone and gave him a piece of her mind, how Granny
had had to call emergencies because of her heart and so on.
He just hung up and Mum didn't even give Granny a
chance to talk to her darling boy.*

*5 January. Lena came to the tutorial before dialectical
materialism and told me that it hadn't worked out with t
he fancy dress ball, on 30 December she'd gone and taken*

*herself off to some aunt of hers in Leningrad and all she'd done was sit and watch telly with a whole bunch of relatives including a load of little children who all started crying because they had to go to bed. The whole world weeping and quarrelling on New Year's Eve! S. wasn't at the tutorial.*

*8 January. I got a C and will have to resit. There was great uproar at home because my grant might be taken away. S. turned up, got an A as usual and left. Lena said she'd rung S. and he'd spent New Year's with some old schoolmates of his. Lena said S. was probably queer and we both had a good laugh.*

*12 January. S. turned up to work at the library with T.I. from the third year who everyone knows is a prostitute. They kept smiling at each other, then S. stood up, went up behind her and put his jacket over her shoulders. He was left wearing just his black sweater. Lena was sitting there with a forced smile, she had red blotches all over her cheeks. Then we went to the toilets to have a smoke and she started crying. I didn't cry, I felt so empty inside. In the immortal words, life on this earth is very dull, gentlemen. I love you, S. Although you don't even notice me. I want to give him a photo of me with just one word: 'Remember'. But how? T.I. is an old prostitute, she's twenty already. I was seventeen in December. S. will be seventeen in February, he went to school when he was six. You can't help comparing. Lena's nineteen. Lena's a good friend, but she's too big, which is going to make life difficult for her. She's gone on a diet. She's got spots on her forehead. I sometimes get them round my nostrils. And she smokes far too much! She's never said anything to me, but she's already been with boys. She told me she knows just as much as T.I., all the different positions and so on. S. isn't a real man, she's convinced of it.*

**15 January.** In bed. For lack of anything better to do I'm pretending to study and instead writing down the conversation between Mum and Granny.

'You? You've already broken all the dishes!' (That's Mum.)

'What dishes? You must be mad!' Granny screams. 'What have I broken, where? Ooh, you'll make me die of fright!'

'Look at that cup, you've broken the handle off! Where am I going to buy another one? Where am I going to get new plates?'

'It wasn't me, it wasn't! Lord help me! Save me! Oh my God! What's happening to me! Lord, people, save me! I'll swear on bended knee it wasn't me! (judging from the noise this takes a good long time). There! I swear!'

'O-o-o-oh, get up, get up, there's no need for all this, if you broke it you broke it.'

(Long-drawn-out moan): 'Save me, everyone! But where . . . where . . . (judging from the groans, she's trying to get up) . . . what did I break?! (In tears.) When you broke my blue cup . . . '

'That's right, that's right, and let's remember your unhappy childhood too . . . '

'The only thing I did break was the teapot spout . . . (sound of chair scraping. Obviously she's sitting down for a cup of tea). I admit, that was me, but you can easily stick it on again . . . I hid the spout . . . '

'Which teapot?!!!'

'The spout of the blue teapot, that's all it was. It'll stick back on again – what's all the fuss about?'

'Which . . . what!!! Oh my God! This is the best yet! She's ruined the tea set! Broken the spout! Our best teapot! How's it ever going to pour again now?! Oh-oh-oh!' (Bursts into tears.)

*'You broke the cup, I broke the spout.'*
*'Al-yona! Come here.'*
*'I've got exams, Mum.'*
End of diary.

Just to finish her off completely, I return to the
theme of spots.

'About your spots, incidentally,' I went on, 'you
know if you don't wash properly, especially down
here and under your arms, and if you don't wash
your knickers out, you get not just smelly but spotty
into the bargain. You ought to wash them yourself!
I end up doing the washing for both of you; fine,
Grandma's off her trolley, but you!'

'I'm off my trolley too,' came the reply from my
(just slightly) spotty girl, pale as death like a
Turgenev heroine. Everyone was supposed to be at
her feet, everyone! But the least she could do was
wash herself.

'The least you can do is take a bath and wash your
hair, that's the first thing. And the other is you've
got to take precautions, you must take precautions if
you're already going round sleeping with all and
sundry.'

By this time she was already in her room having a
good weep over herself, thank God. Oh the egoism
of youth! I was honestly afraid she'd be so shaken by
the sight of her grandmother she'd stop sleeping all
over again, but wounding words have such power to
revive!

This was all well over seven years ago – a lifetime.

*

Night.

Just today there was a ring at the doorbell. As always I called out: 'Who's there?' Answer: 'Open up.'

Charming! For whom? (All this through the door.) Then:

'Does So-and-So live here?'

The name of my dear son. In a voice with a heavy accent.

No. No, no, no.

'Then where can I find him, Missus?'

I got a terrible fright. I told the voice he was renting a flat somewhere.

'Address.' Not likely! How should I know? 'Open up.' No, I said, I'm not obliged to open the door to anyone without a warrant. Silence. Okay, love, but I'd advise your son to take very good care of himself. Where are you from, the prison? Criminals, are you? 'No, love, it's him that's the criminal, get it? And we're going to find him and get him no matter what, so you better look out.' Then came a volley of kicks at the door, kicks from a good many feet. At least six. I didn't venture out that day but called Andrei straight away. Evidently His Royal Highness was out of sorts. His answers were monosyllables at best.

'Hello.'

' . . . '

'How's your foot?'

'Nnnn.'

'Have you found a job yet?'

'Nnnn.'

'Why not?'

'Go — your mother.'

'You're addressing the wrong person. With the best will in the world I can't do what you suggest with my mother – your grandmother. Come on, cheer up! What's the matter with you?'

'Ah . . . mmm.'

'You must find a job.'

' . . . '

'And by the way, someone's out hunting for you again.'

'Who? You mean my friends want to see me?'

'That's right, your friends. They told me they'll find you no matter what. They're out to get you, they said.'

'Who?'

'Friends of yours, as you say yourself. I told them: Get out, you bunch of criminals.'

'Oh yeah?' (Threateningly.)

'And they said: How can you be so sure who the criminals are? What have you gone and done this time, Andrei?'

'Me? What d'you mean? Why me?'

Judging from his answer there really was something.

'Anyway, they're after you, there were at least six feet outside the door. Judging by the racket they made.'

'Three of them?'

'You'd know better than me. Maybe there were six of them, all one-legged. The point is they're out for you, so don't go coming round here.'

'Huh. I wanted to get some money off you.'

'You – off me?'

'You've just made the whole thing up, haven't you, Mum?'

'Lunatic,' I said and hung up. He's already exacted twice over the monthly tribute I'm supposed to pay him, for some unknown reason! Robbed twice over! Completely destitute! And the first time, to add insult to injury, he stole a precious book of mine, a children's book, *Little Lord Fauntleroy*. I'd been waiting all this time for Tima to get over his horror at the news that the poor little Lord wouldn't be left a penny. Once, just once, I'd started reading it to him, but that was as far as we got, he wouldn't let me go any further, so I put the book aside, and now Andrei's gone and stolen it. Imagine my panic! The only thing Tima's forbidden to do is unlock my bookcase.

Humiliating negotiations. The kid and I went and stood guard outside the hospital early one morning after Andrei's wife Nina had finished her shift. Nina was grumpy and gloomy and said she couldn't live with him any more, he had to leave. Eventually it emerged they hadn't paid the rent for six whole months. Nina had somehow managed to pay the telephone bill, but the electricity had been cut off. At this point in despair Andrei had come and robbed me.

Nina agreed to exchange *Little Lord Fauntleroy* for forty roubles. Forty roubles! I'd always suspected Nina was one of those two tarts in the dark glasses and fancy dress, I've never trusted her.

That was the last time Andrei visited the maternal nest in my absence. I went out of my way after that to put in an extra lock, it was a great to-do, I had to find a locksmith and in the end two of them turned up, took a thorough look at the door, the hall wallpaper, the floor, what can you do. The door wasn't right, according to them, the lock 'wouldn't take', but I begged them, told them the whole truth: there was a man registered at the apartment who was just out of prison and was trying to break in and steal everything I had. He couldn't get work, he had nothing to eat, and as for me . . . I didn't cry, but I was trembling all over. They lost interest at this point; their usual ploy – the game they always play making out they can't carry out the work without some extra money, the eternal struggle for a few extra roubles – had run aground this time on the evident grief of a stranger. They left, I collapsed on my bed in the safety of my new fortress, but my peace was short-lived. Andrei was determined to milk me dry this time. We spent that month in a feverish whirl. I asked Burkin, the head of department, for an extra forty letters to answer, saying I was up to my ears in debt, and that hit home because he'd been in debt himself. He was deaf to all other pleas – births, illnesses, prisons, he couldn't stand hearing about them, refused to react. But cash for a drink or two – that struck a sympathetic chord. Hard truths about my life just made him uneasy, and I was always so bouncy when I went to the office! I literally fluttered in, smiling all over and scattering compliments about, my cheeks shone, my face, I could feel it, grew tighter over my cheekbones, and I always gave my hands a good going-over in advance – my poor hands, my pair of rakes, rough as a tortoise's – I cut the nails round like little brackets, gave my skin a good massage. During these visits to the journal offices the kid had to be put out to graze, I left him down on the little divan near the doorman – children aren't allowed upstairs. Upstairs, on the third floor, I was an unjustly neglected poetess, and my alcoholic boss was my patron, stern but fair. Just as Chekhov said, Burkin had to squeeze the slave from himself drop by drop – in other words, he'd never give in straight away to my flattery: 'What would I do without you,' I'd say, or 'Just a little kopeck for a nice cup of vodka', or 'You're my saviour'. He'd burrow in his desk, wander out, you could hear the empty bottle rolling round in his drawer, a useless hint as far as I was concerned, I never give bribes and I've nothing to give them with anyway; then he'd ring someone up, dig in his briefcase, various girls would come in to see him, they'd arrive one by one but then gather round in a little knot and refuse to leave, everyone seemed to be waiting for something. They'd sit on his desk, sit virtually in his lap, all of them young and beautiful, and all the while Tima was languishing downstairs, waiting for me, twisting himself upside down from boredom. At this point various businesslike men from some other department would invariably turn up, but of course that wasn't what everyone was waiting for, they were all hoping to be taken off somewhere for a drink. And I had only one thing on the brain: letters, letters, letters!

Quite possibly the girls were on the lookout for letters too, maybe they were all hungry poets as well, but Burkin couldn't feed the lot of them, he also gave letters to the widow of a friend of his who'd drowned, his body had never been found and there'd been problems over the pension, he left two small children and a wife who didn't work and couldn't do anything to save her skin. The boss taught her to fire off five types of standard answer on the stencil, she admitted it to me herself, whereas I'd compose veritable works of art to cover every need, each one unique, I'd spend mad nights conversing with the invisible souls of pensioners, sailors, accounts clerks, students and schoolchildren, foremen, doctors, nightwatchmen and prisoners. She would write: 'Dear Comrade . . . Unfortunately, your poem(s), story (ies), novel, novella, epic poem is/are not of interest to the editorial board of our journal. The particular themes of our journal are such-and-such.' That was variant no. 1. And if in fact they'd written on the appropriate theme, she put: 'Your work leaves something to be desired in terms of style and language. With all best wishes . . . '

As for me, I wrote whole poems. I quoted, advised, praised and criticised with utmost sympathy. Burkin would take these works of mine and look positively ill when he read them. But behind every one of these manuscripts I saw real people, some of them sick, some of them perhaps even bedridden like Nikolai Ostrovsky! Cripples and hunchbacks! Sometimes they'd start writing to me personally and sending their manuscripts to me to review, but when this happened Burkin would invariably hand their letters over to the poor widow instead.

Burkin feared new authors like the plague.


I've just written a strange piece taking on the persona of my daughter, something like an extract from her memoirs, it's wonderful what can come over you in the middle of the night sitting sleepless in the kitchen. Here's an extract, pray God Burkin never sees it:

*It's better out on the street, better to be as I am now, what with the owner of the apartment, one Sheremetiev, giving me the place while he went to make a pile in Siberia and then coming back on a visit, he found a crack at the base of the toilet and said, 'I've come back, I'll be having my lady friends round here, nowhere else to go, can't take them to my wife's, a powerful man like me has his needs, you and the kid better go off somewhere, or you can stay if you like, it sometimes works in a threesome.'*

Author's note: the terrible things that come into one's head, awful, awful, imagining my daughter so vulnerable, but that was virtually what she burst out with one day, in floods of tears, that's what she said her life was like. She told me everything about Sheremetiev.

The text continues:

*Once I spent the night at Mum's with the baby; in the middle of the night I suddenly heard a great din and hullabaloo, she turned on all the lights and made a great scene of taking the boy to have a pee: 'Have a good old wee, then, now you've gone and wet yourself anyway.' She switched on the light in our room and started rootling round in the cupboard for fresh pants. Katya woke up in her crib and the boy was standing there barefoot, clutching her elbow with two skinny hands and trembling from cold, just in his vest with no pants, having wet himself. His thin little bottom, his skinny legs, a mass of tousled curls on his* head and down to his shoulders, a little angel! Wouldn't even look at us, and there was Katya lying in her crib grunting away, I had to get up anyway but wished I didn't.

'Mum,' I said, 'let me help, I'll find them.'

'What'll you find?' – Cries, shrieks, tears – 'What do you know about anything here? Blasted idiot! Bastard! Brat! (It's not clear who this is addressed to.) How many times do I have to tell you not to drink before bedtime! And you, living off our money! You might have the decency not to eat what's his so he goes drinking out of hunger!' (She stands there, statuesque still, in a torn nightie, tearing her elbow away from his little pincers. Suddenly he bursts into bitter sobs and covers his face with his hands.) 'There!' she screams, like some Ancient Greek goddess of horror. 'There! Put them on!'

'Come here, sweetheart, let me put them on for you,' I said, lacking the strength to get up off my backside.

'Let him do it himself, let him do it himself, he's out on his own now, I'm headed for the knacker's yard and there's no one left to look after him! He'll just have to look after himself!'

Suddenly, as if from a blow, he fell to the floor sobbing. What a scene! And then my Katya started up, and how she yelled and yelled!

That's the scene I wrote – fully self-critical, completely objective, though why on earth you might well ask.

The thing was that out of the blue, for about the first time in a year, she decides to ring up. There she is living, as we know, out in some godforsaken place in the outskirts with her fat little bastard of a daughter brought into this world thanks to that blighter she'd supposedly set up home with. So suddenly we're talking and just as suddenly it's all over, I didn't have time to collect myself and answer back properly. This is how it went (just imagine) . . .

The phone rings: *drring! drring!*

The kid rushes up but I beat him to it, there's a momentary struggle for the receiver.

'Hello!'

'It's me, Mum.'

'Greetings!' (I say.)

'Okay, okay.'

'Okay meaning what?'

'Mum, listen. I've got protein in my urine.'

'How many times have I told you to be more strict about your hygiene! You don't wash yourself properly, that's all your protein's about.'

By way of reply I hear strained laughter. As always, in fact. When she's about ready to die she gives this strained laugh. Wait till we see who gets the last laugh though.

'Mum.'

'All right, all right, I'm listening.'

'Tell me what to do. They want to put me in hospital.'

'Don't talk nonsense. You've got a baby, for God's sake, how on earth can you go into hospital? Now go and give yourself a good wash and then give them a proper sample.'

Answer:

'Okay, forget it. But what if I really do have bad blood? What does it mean? Am I going to die?'

'Now what's all this about bad blood? In this day

and age! Who d'you suppose has got good blood? Tima? You're his mother, do you have even the remotest idea what it means that he's got such-and-such haemoglobin when the norm is such-and-such?'

Strained laughter.

'I've got half that' (she replies).

'I'm not talking about you! I'm talking about your son, your son's life! Do something about it, at least pay up! Give back the money you went and grabbed! Go on, do it! Pay up at least! He needs liver to eat! Walnuts! Stop giggling now, there's nothing funny about it, you rotten bitch! She-devil!'

'Okay. So, Mum, so you don't think there's anything serious?'

'Now what are you sobbing about?' (Pause.)

'I'm not sobbing.' (Stifled laughter.)

'Who is, then?'

'Listen.' (Her voice trembling.) 'Listen. They're putting me in hospital to keep me under observation.'

'What? What's all this nonsense! You're deranged. What was that you said?!'

'The baby's due in two weeks, and they say if you've got high blood pressure it means, you know, you can die of a coma or something. While you're in labour. You get convulsions and things. My kidneys'll pack up and that'll be it. What am I going to do with Katya?'

'Ts ts ts. Calm down, they tried to scare me with all this stuff as well. But you can't scare our family. When Andrei was little and I was pregnant with you they said the same thing to me. What of it? They

96

couldn't care less that I was a mother already, and of course that famous father of yours . . . I never set foot inside a hospital, I just checked in normally when the contractions started, it was half-past six in the morning, I woke him up . . . '

'Okay then.'

'Your dear father wouldn't even get out of bed . . . don't swallow the bait, there's no need to go! They'll have you on a table in a trice and start tinkering inside you with a spoon for their so-called analyses and then you'll give birth prematurely like I did: they went and made my waters break! It's to their advantage if you give birth ahead of time, they don't have to pay so much maternity leave then, and what do the doctors care?'

'Then I'll do what you say, Mum, in any case I'd talked it over with a neighbour and she said she could have Katya for exactly five days, no more, but she'd never have her for the two weeks extra.'

'Well then, you just hold on, bear up, what else can you do! If you keep out of their way they can't force you into hospital. There's nothing to worry about.'

'Okay then, 'bye.'

'Bye. Kisses.'

'Ugh-huh . . . oh (laughter), how's the kid?'

'What's that to you?' (Triumphantly.)

At which point I put the phone down.


And only then came to. Only then did the meaning of the whole thing become menacingly clear, only then did I realise the full horror of my position.

97

First, she was having another baby.

Second, she'd said goodbye and wandered off somewhere, pregnant, and with her pram into the bargain, wanting – obviously – to leave the fat creature with me. For God knows how long. What was I to do, Lord, what was I to do? What had got into her deranged female brain this time? What did she want to go having another child for? How had she managed to miss the boat this time, why didn't she have an abortion? It was clear as daylight: she'd come to and realised only when the creature started kicking inside her, I could just picture the whole thing. When a mother's still feeding she quite often misses periods anyway, misses 'the Red Army' as she used to say to her Lena: 'The Red Army's arrived, I can't do PE today.' Lots of women fall into that trap. The male climbs aboard and what does he care? But which one was it this time? Who did it? That same stray Deputy Director or some passing handyman? Or – worse and worse – her landlord from Siberia? And how long was all this going to go on? Obviously they refused to give her a late abortion. So after that (I fit the pieces together) she starts going to the doctors with her counterindications, her protein and high blood pressure, hoping in vain they'd do the abortion anyway, and – hop! They'd got her on the line, all they had to do now was reel her in and pop her in hospital for investigation and not let her out again, as if they couldn't risk letting slip a single baby. You'd think they really needed all these babies. It's the usual thing, the professionals getting carried away, hooked on their own game like chess players. Not for any good reason but just because that's the procedure. Save the child at all costs. But who and what for? She should have found the right person to do it! Get a woman to give her the injection, a woman doctor, you can always talk the women into it even as late as six months. Andrei's wife Nina was telling about one of her neighbours who'd failed to get her abortion done in time, she'd wasted precious time, gone off to the seaside and let the moment slip, so she ends up sending her kids off somewhere for the weekend – it was October by this time, freezing cold outside – gets herself an injection and fetches up giving birth to a six-month-old foetus, a boy, he kept mewing the whole night by an open window while she washed the floors in the next room – ow – ow – ow – but by morning he fell silent, as she'd counted on. It went on the whole night and she never once went up to him. And the doctor did nothing to help, just ran off after giving the injection. So there you are: if she'd found a doctor, even a man, and just paid him to do it . . . Why drink our blood for nothing? Why didn't she take care? Is her mother supposed to bear the brunt for everyone?

The whole conversation had nothing to do with protein and urine, what the whole conversation amounted to was this: Mummy, help me, hoist just one more burden on your back, you've always come to my rescue before, rescue me now – But, daughter, I haven't the strength to love yet another creature, I'd be betraying the boy, he couldn't take it, as it is he looked pretty murderously at his sister. – But what am I to do, Mum? – Nothing, I can't do any more to help, I've given you everything, my darling, all the money I have, my darling, my sunshine – I'm going to die,

Mum, it's terrible – No, my darling, you must be strong. Look at me, I force myself to be strong, I just keep going because I'm your mother, I'm all you have. Not long ago a funny thing happened: a man in the street started pestering me, mistook me for a girl! 'Hey, miss!' he called me. Can you imagine? Your mother's still a woman, you know! You must be strong. All right? You can't live here, it'll just be the same thing all over again – faces contorted with hatred, glowering at each other from the mirror in the hall, we always have our rows there, always fight it out in the hall, it's the springboard for every battle. And He's forever beside us, the holy child, who can't yet grasp that the world about him is about to cave in, his Mummy (me) and his Alyona (his mother), his two heroines, are locked in final combat, saying the unsayable. And he's all I live for! You said yourself that it was better to be out on the streets than living with me! Be strong, my daughter! – All right, Mum, forgive me, I'm a fool. I kiss you. (That anyway was how I mentally continued the conversation.)

The kid came up to me and said, 'Grandma, why are you shaking like that? Take your hands off your face and stop shaking, eh? Don't be mad.' – And at last the glad tears gushed from my eyes, from those dry gullies, burst out like sunshine through rain in the birchwoods, my darling, my sun that never sets.

His face like a dead man's lay still under my endless kisses. His skin is pale and shiny, his eyelashes thick and sticky, spread like rays of sunshine on his cheeks, his eyes grey with a spot of dark blue like Granny Sima's. Mine are golden, the colour of honey. What a beauty you are, my angel!

100

'Who were you talking to?'

'It doesn't matter, little one. My beauty.'

'No, but who?'

'I told you, it was just grown-up business.'

'Was it Alyona? Were you shouting at her?'

I felt uncomfortable before my angel. Children are conscience personified. They pose their little questions anxiously, like angels, then suddenly stop asking and turn into adults. Plug up their doubts and start living their lives. That's when they realise how helpless they are. They can't do anything about it all, and neither can anyone else. But how can I play tricks on him? Can't do it.

'Why were you shouting that she ought to wash herself?'

'Of course I wasn't, darling! I was just telling her she ought to wash the floor.'

'Are you mad?'

'Yes, my angel, completely mad, a total idiot. I love you.'


Endless fluttery kisses on his cheeks, his little brow, his nose – never on the lips. You should never kiss children on the lips. Once I saw a man with his little girl on the tram, no doubt collecting her from kindergarten. And he was pestering her to death with his kisses, right on the lips. I told him off sharply right in front of everyone else. He started as if caught red-handed, all crimson and agitated, and his poor little girl, about five years old, was completely overcome with all the giggling and tickling

101

– he'd been tickling her as well. He came to and started cursing me filthily, looking at me with hurt hunted eyes. How could he have known? He said what everyone else says: Stop bloody meddling in other people's business.

'Look what you're doing to the child!' I said. 'I can just imagine what you get up to with her at home! Don't you know it's a crime!'

The whole tram started bristling, but against me, not him.

'What business is it of yours, you old ( . . . )! An old bag like you still trying to stick your oar in!'

'My sole concern is the well-being of your child. People can be imprisoned for that, you know. Depraved acts with minors! Raping children!'

'Bloody madwoman! Cretin!'

'Just you wait till she's twelve and suddenly, hey presto, she's pregnant! And not by you either!'

Thank God I'd managed to distract him – now he was consumed by quite another desire: to knock me unconscious on the spot. Maybe now every time he starts subjecting his daughter to caresses he'll remember me and switch to hating instead. And I will have saved another child! I spend my whole life saving children! I'm the only one in the entire neighbourhood who stays alert at night, listening and listening to make sure no one's crying out! Once at three in the morning one summer night I heard a stifled cry: 'My God, what are you doing! My God, what is this!' The helpless muffled half-scream of a woman. My hour had struck: I leaned out of the window and bellowed majestically: '*What* is going on! I'll call the police.'

(As a matter of fact the police are usually quite eager to intervene in such cases where the felon's still on the spot: a hundred per cent success, catching him in the act! I know this from my own research.)

Someone immediately stuck their nose out of another window, lower down. I heard another shout, and just two minutes later two people came running to help. My sole aim was to scare him off, get him to drop her before he did anything.

'Yes, yes, comrades, he's here, over here, in the bushes!' (despite the fact they still had a hundred yards or so to run).

In an instant he jumped out of the bushes and was off in a flash round the corner. At which point the woman in the bushes burst into noisy sobs. I could just imagine the horror and loathing, being stifled by bestial hands and shoved against the wall.

I remember myself the sickening sensation of feeling a stranger's hands suddenly start twitching up my side in the Metro, like a snake slithering into my insides: someone was crudely fumbling with my handbag. I turned round and shouted 'Are you the one rummaging in my handbag!' And three of the people round me, a giggling woman and two swarthy characters with shaved heads, made off quickly along with my man, the perpetrator – likewise shaved and swarthy – and disappeared in the crowd. Little by little, that's how to defeat them!

Bringing enlightenment, the light of the law, to these benighted folk, these swarming masses! The dark conscience incarnate of simple people speaks within me and I'm no longer myself, I'm an oracle,

I lay down the law! The children who hear me speak – in schools, in summer camps, in clubs – they all shrink and tremble, but they never forget!

And then my little one, my grief, is always beside me, I sometimes forget he's there and the children look now at him, now at me, absorbing us both as a single indivisible entity. Afterwards they pay me seven roubles odd, but if I get three to four readings plus the letters . . .

What power in the world can stop a woman who has to feed her child! What power in the whole world!

This week, thanks to Nadya B. – she's arranged a couple of these things for me – I'm giving a reading at a children's winter camp. So we make the journey out there, the gathering's due to take place at the Propaganda Bureau and they said they'd feed us as well!!! As always I drag Tima along. It takes an age to get ready, we have the usual quarrel over clothes.

And that was when the worst began – not the worst in itself, but the beginning of everything that came afterwards. The telephone rang, the kid rushed up and got there first and stood there for ages pressing the receiver to his head with both hands, refusing to let go – the usual story, he always rushes to grab the phone.

'Hello! Hello!' he says. 'What? Who? Anna what? Hello! Who d'you want?'

'Give it to me darling, give Grandma the phone.'

'Hold on! I can't hear anything! What, hello!' (Silence.)

They've hung up.

Me: 'Never do that again! Do you hear me? Never . . .'

The phone rings again, and again we struggle. I grab the receiver, he roars and starts kicking me in the shins. Painfully . . . I manage to shove him away and continue talking politely while the kid sits there on the floor, his eyes flashing like crystal – now he's gathering breath, gasping for air, three-two-one-zero and off we go! *A-a-a-a-h!!!*

'Just a moment, please. Either you shut up . . .'

'*Aaaaaah!*'

Neither Alyona nor Andrei was ever as bad as this when they were little, it's because of his encephalitis, his mother must have dropped him from the table when he was a baby, I'd warned her about it before, his nerves are completely shattered, he's like an hysterical old woman.

Meanwhile down the phone a polite little provincial voice is informing me that my mother, Serafima Georgievna, is being transferred from hospital to an institution for chronic psychotics.

So that's that, I thought. That's that. My worst fears come true. And the doctor knows, she knows very well that I've nowhere to put my mother at home, she knows what I live on.

'Excuse me, dear, what was your name again?'

'Well – Valya, you can call me Valya.'

'Valya dear, what's all this about? What's happened? Hasn't she been behaving herself? Where's Miriam Abramovna?'

'Miriam Abramovna's on leave, all of us are on leave from the first of the month . . . they're carrying out a refurbishment and all the patients are being sent to different places; those that can do are going home, the others – the ones who don't have family or where no one wants to have them – are being put in institutions. Some are going to another hospital. But your – your aunt, is she? – Your mother . . . '

'It doesn't matter if she's my aunt or my mother, she's a human being . . . '

'They won't take the old lady anywhere else.'

'But why, Valya dear? What's the problem?'

'We can't keep her here.'

'Maybe I should drop in and talk it over with someone? Who's there at the moment? Wait a minute, darling, this isn't for you' (he takes a running jump at me and delivers two blows on the kidneys). 'Heavens, Valya, what's the problem? Valya dear?'

'Well it's up to you. The forms are all ready for the institution. Don't you worry, there's really no need for you to come, we've dealt with all the formalities. They're moving her there tomorrow.'

'I see . . . Hush, darling' (I had him by the shirt-tails but he's slithered out of my grasp). 'Why such a hurry?'

Feverishly I try to work out what to do. So, they're moving her, and the state will take away her pension. If you're put in an institution you don't get any-thing. So now we're completely in the soup. Completely. As it happens, her pension's due in two days' time – will I still be able to get it? Maybe they won't pay up. Oh my goodness, what misery! You don't have a bean but somehow you make ends meet – until they deliver the final blow that makes you feel you've been living in clover till then. Misery, misery.

106

They die like flies in those institutions.

'What do you mean hurry, there's been no particular hurry about it.' The voice resurfaces suddenly. 'We've given you due warning. And there's nothing to worry about!'

'For a start nobody gave me any warning at all. What institution are you taking her to, where?'

'Now don't you worry. It's out of town. But we'll transport her, it's all been arranged.'

'So now I'm supposed to travel out of town every time, two hours each way, thanks very much.'

'Well in fact it's a little further than that, but why do you need to go there at all?' says Valya. 'They've got everything there she needs. Anyway, I've warned you. The only thing, though, is that we need your signature, but that can wait.'

'What am I supposed to sign?'

'Your consent.'

'But I don't consent, what do you mean!'

'Well, will you take her home then?'

'You won't get any signatures from me,' I say furiously, 'not one! The idea of it!'

And I put the phone down.

As always, we have a quarrel about his clothes; the boy refuses to put on his felt boots and galoshes and he doesn't want the nice fur hat with earflaps – once upon a time it was Andrei's – he'll only wear the light knitted one.

But it's freezing cold! What are you doing to me, do you want to fall sick again and have me watch over you day and night? I beg you on bended knee, darling, etcetera, etcetera. In the end we set off without the earflaps but with the felt boots; it was a good compromise – 'You can keep your head in the cold if your feet are in the warm,' as the saying goes. It's only seven minutes' walk to the Metro if you go briskly, the Metro's nice and warm, and after that it's three stops on the bus. A heap of money to spend on tickets, but they were taking us the rest of the way by car, a draughty green jeep as it happened. Better than nothing, anyway. A lady I'd never met before turned out to be coming with us, she was clad in a fancy sheepskin torn at the back seams and a home-made fox-fur hat.

'Your coat's split at the back, the sleeve . . . '

'Oh dear, is it? I'm forever mending it . . . '

Trying to swan it like the rest of us, but she'll give her performance for tuppence halfpenny just like me. The lowest rate.

'I'm a poet, what about you?' I asked, just to get our specialities straight.

'Me?' says Fox Fur. 'They call me a folk story-teller.'

'I'm sorry?'

'A folk storyteller: I tell them fairy tales and do little shows with dolls.'

'Dolls?'

'Oh, it's nothing special really, I make these funny little dolls – out of potatoes and hemp and all sorts of things. Your little girl will enjoy it.'

I see, so she can't even tell the difference between a boy and a girl, though I must admit everyone's confused by Tima's curls. My little girl stares with swollen eyes out of the window; he's taken his hat off in the freezing cold.

'Well, I'm a poet,' I tell her. 'Put that hat back on,

108

do you hear me, put it back on! It's funny, you know,
I'm the namesake, almost, of a famous poet . . .
Otherwise we can't go on, I'll tell the driver to stop
right here and leave us in the road, now put it on.'
   'Which poet?,' the storyteller asks reasonably.
   'Guess. My name's Anna Andrianovna . . . it's like
a sign from above.'
   'Ah, there's always something mystical in names.
Take mine, for instance . . . Xenia.'
   'What in particular . . . ?'
   'It means stranger. A stranger to the world.'
   'Ah . . . well, yes, quite a name to be landed with.'
   'Uh-huh . . . '
Silence. There's a howling emptiness in my stomach and in my soul – I don't know if it's true for
everyone, but my soul is located just above my stomach, between my ribs. I feel the alarm signal go off
right there. I've had nothing to eat at all, what with
the call from the hospital I didn't have a second,
I'd tried to get hold of a psychiatrist I'd met ages
ago but when I rang his home number all I was told
(in a tone of utmost bitterness) was 'They don't
live here any more'. Must have been some dreadful
family row, obviously there was no point asking for
his new number. I got Tima fed, sprinkled a lump of
bread with some sugar for him and gave him some
cold tea, he likes that, the little piglet, crunched
away and got all covered in crumbs. This 'patry' of
his comes flavoured with my tears. I can see very well
he's hungry too, but before we get to eat anything
we've got to shudder along in the jeep, it's cold and
stinks of kerosene from some kind of sacking at the
back, oh cold and bitter fate! At least for today

Mother's still in the hospital (I rang back and couldn't get hold of any Valya at all, there was no one of that name working there, they said, another complete mystery); anyway, Mother is there and eating well – I know that, having seen her at it – greedily sucking in her thin ragged lips, champing toothlessly away, her eyes dull and lustreless, the pupils misted over as if stamped on her eyeballs: a tiny round dull stamp. I remember the way she lay there the last time, her shoulders nothing but bones, the tears running down from wide-open eyes and trickling over her temples. How can they take her anywhere in that state, the swine, can't she be left in peace to die where she is! But no. Revenge for all our deeds overtakes us all in the end, when we're so wretched there's nothing left to take vengeance on. Vengeance on whom? But there, right at the end, they won't leave you in peace. It's very odd, though, I wonder who this Valya was? Where was she ringing from? Or were they just too lazy at the hospital to go and find her? I'd called three times – twice they said 'Hold on' and then the phone went completely dead till I hung up in despair.

'Children are the best listeners of all,' this Xenia was saying.

'Of course they are,' I agreed.

'You turn up and there's a great hubbub going on, but as soon as the performance starts . . . ' She has to shout at the top of her voice; the jeep jolts over the bumps and potholes, the motor roars.

Maybe Andrei's wife was playing some trick on me? Did she hire a friend to do it? No. It was all confirmed. Tomorrow Mother would be discharged, tomorrow.

' . . . folk tales,' concludes Xenia.

'What's your patronymic, may I ask?'

'Just call me Xenia.'

'I'd feel awkward . . . with a pensioner, after all
. . . '

'Pensioner? I'm not a pensioner,' answers the
fatherless lady, who's obviously old enough to be a
grandmother herself.

'Well, I am,' I tell her. 'If my book of verse comes
out, the pension will have to be adjusted, I ought to
get more. In the meantime Tima and I live God
knows how, and now my mother's being discharged
from hospital, my daughter can't go out to work,
she's been left with two small children on her hands
and just the alimony, and my son's disabled' (I list
all my woes like a beggar on the train).

'Well,' says my fatherless companion, bouncing
over the bumpy road alongside us, 'well, I've just
won a car in a lottery. I'm learning to drive.'

'Oh really. Yes, I've heard of people buying up
these winning lottery tickets, claiming they're the
winners, and it all ends up in court with them
stripped of their so-called winnings.'

'We have a son,' she tells me, this lady who can't
remember her father, her cheeks wobbling from the
speed and the bumps. 'We need to be able to drive
him to his music lessons, so it'll come in very handy.
My husband doesn't drive on principle, it was my
mother bought the lottery ticket.'

'I see, you started late on family life,' I say. 'But
never mind, he'll be grown-up by the time you're
eighty-odd.'

'Mummy!' says Tima – he sometimes calls me

'Mummy', sometimes 'Grandma'. 'Mummy! I'm hungry!'

'Would your little girl – is she your daughter? – would she like a sweetie?' mumbles our companion, the stranger to the world.

He gobbles it down like a dog – gulp! Then he looks at her hopefully again.

'Say thank you and put on your hat, then the nice lady might give you another one,' I say.

Tima just sits there, not quite able to believe me.

'Look at you with your hat off,' I say. 'If you go falling ill again and I've got Granny coming home from hospital . . . tomorrow . . . whoops (we fly in the air) – I'm going to fetch Granny home. Remember Granny Sima? (Forestalling his question: 'Who's this other granny you're talking about?') 'Granny Sima wouldn't let you go out without a hat! God forbid! Now put it back on.'

The nice lady mumbles:

'Yes indeed, I always keep a store of them . . . I suffer from a stomach ulcer . . . mother gets us imported ones, she's always pressing them on us . . . '

Go on then, give one to the child!

'So now then' (I say), 'one, two, three and on it goes!' I put the hat on him. Tima and I exchange meaning looks. Tima says nothing.

Some people have all the luck, I think to myself. You can just imagine the mother. Lottery tickets, a car, imported sweets . . .

Tima cautiously raises a hand to his hat.

'No, Tima, don't take it off!'

So embarrassing. Fatherless Xenia has fallen into a reverie, head bowed and shaking like a jelly. There are people around who can kill you with a flick of the wrist, you have to dance on all fours before them to earn a single glance, they never look you in the face, let alone smile. Just gaze past you thoughtfully.

'Is he allowed chocolate? I know some children aren't; my son never is.'

'No, no, we don't give him chocolate,' I say.

Tima sits frozen still, to the extent you can in a bouncing car.

'What a pity, the chocolates are all I have left.'

'He shouldn't really, thanks all the same – otherwise, you know – it brings on a rash.' Got to take a firm stance. We're not beggars!

Tima's eyes, by now out on stalks, brim over at this point – diamonds of pure water. Now the tears are going to flow, pauper's tears. He turns away, ashamed. Good lad! That's the way to awaken pride! His little hand reaches out for mine and squeezes it violently.

The nice lady delicately pops another sweet in her mouth.

'I'm not allowed to go for long intervals without eating.'

'Well now, let's bend the rules a little,' I say. 'Just this once we'll allow him one. One a day can't do him any harm, especially as it's not real chocolate, they're mostly soya mix these days. It's years since we had real chocolate. They keep reducing the percentage . . . '

Tima champs away just like his great-grandmother, unrestrained, almost choking for joy. The emptiness howls in my stomach like wind in the chimney.

They greet us warmly at the children's camp.

'Would you like a cup of tea before we begin? The children have just had theirs.'

It's dark already, the yellow streetlamps lit, the air intoxicating, dusted with frost.

'I'm not sure . . . I need to do a bit of preparation,' I say.

But Xenia, our fatherless friend, insists:

'What do you mean! We have plenty of time! We must have a nice hot cup of tea if we're going to be speaking! It's good for the voice!'

We sit down at a table in the huge canteen, I drink tea and eat a toffee and help myself to two stout slices of bread – they always cut the bread here in chunks from round loaves, and bread's what I love most, can't get enough of it. My nose is running, somewhere in my briefcase among all the manuscripts I've got a clean boiled rag but I can't seem to find it, I blow my nose daintily on a scrap of paper – they have torn-up scraps of paper here instead of napkins. Somewhere in the distance there's a babble of children, they're bringing them into the auditorium now, Xenia and I dash into the toilet, she lifts up her skirt and starts taking off her woolly breeches and there she is left just in her woolly stockings, I catch a glimpse of bulging belly and stretched knickers. It's awful the way people fail to recognise their own hideousness; often they're quite happy to expose themselves – obese, flabby, grubby and drooping. Beware, all of you; there you go looking like reptiles yet still longing for love! No doubt that man of Xenia's flees from the two of them in horror, her and her mother, and gets his bit on the side for consolation. There's nothing much to be said for old age. Everything droops and wobbles, goes into lumps and globules, veins swollen like ropes. And that's when you're not yet ancient – wait till you turn into yesterday's stale pudding, a lump of old cheese, a vessel of old kvass – as I once wrote long ago in my youth from sheer horror, having glimpsed some old lady's cleavage. Anywhere in the East, no doubt Xenia (and I for that matter) would have been thoroughly packaged up in at least three layers of wrapping, right down to our fingertips and the hennaed soles of our feet. And quite right too!

I did my usual stuff, the children fell quiet, and there I was as always with Tima, he sat next to me at my little table on stage, poured himself some water from the jug, clatter, clatter, slurp, drank a bit of that cold poisonous unboiled stuff and poured the rest back into the jug – let him do what he wants, I say. Although the camp leaders, standing there behind their charges at the back of the hall like kapos in a concentration camp, were already exchanging wary malicious looks. But, as ever, art won the day, I got my round of applause and Tima and I disappeared backstage to await our supper. I tried to get Tima to go back into the hall with the other children to watch Xenia but he wasn't having any of it, wouldn't dream of letting Grandma have a moment's peace to gather her thoughts alone. There among the dust in the darkness he clung to me, jealous and demanding as always, perched on my knees to stare at our story-teller's back. True to her word, she'd poked two eyes in a big potato, stuck the thing on a fork, and with the help of a bit of hemp, a wooden spoon and a pair of washing tongs she made quite an original little show, quite unexpectedly charming. Ah, my friends, the flame of wit still burns in ageing bodies! Just think of my near-namesake, the great poet!

After the story we feasted at a table all to ourselves, the children kept coming up to look at the potato doll and on the sly I managed to slip three big hunks of bread and butter into my bag among the manuscripts, the buttered sides stuck together of course, along with a few toffees; we'd have a sumptuous feast when we got home. I flattered Xenia by asking her if I could take home that great rough thoroughbred potato with the eyes gouged out – she'd obviously bought it at the private market – supposedly so that I could do the same little show again for Tima, but in fact so that we could have a second course! A second course of potato!

So home again, home again. And a joyless awakening next morning after a sleepless night going over and over all the alternatives: a pension's a pension, of course, but the smell of her! The smell! Like in a menagerie. Mother had long since lost control of her functions. How they stank, that wardful of old women, and how ashamed they were in front of strangers, trying to cover themselves up to their chins when they'd soiled themselves up to their chins as well, you should have seen the way one of the nurses whipped the covers off one of them, Krasnova, Mother's neighbour in the ward who'd got herself all cosily tucked in – the heartfelt curses she uttered, the way she shrieked at her, right there in front of me –

how did you manage to get in it up to your neck ugh you filthy old creature! There was a sudden spark in the dull whites of my mother's eyes, you could see them light up with triumph. How well I knew it, that triumphant look! How often I'd glimpsed it through her apparent distress, especially when she'd supposedly been defending me from my husband – anything can happen of course in a family when you live chock-a-block, but God forbid you did anything within sight or earshot of my mother! The triumph of being always right, of being able to say 'I told you so', the triumph of her eternal wisdom against my stupidity.

I've even come to the conclusion that those few kind things she did were done purely to spite someone else, namely me! Many good deeds are done out of sheer contrariness; I dare say the Kid will turn out all kind to his dissolute mother just as a way of getting back at me for always being right – though whether for good or ill, who knows, who knows.

We were well fed that evening: meat and noodles, three glasses of sweet tea, three nice hunks of bread and butter, ah yes – children do pretty well in our country, Tima for that matter used to go to kinder-garten. Those were the days! He got properly fed there, I caught up on sleep, wrote my things, went to the library or the journal offices, even made myself a skirt out of some cheap fabric, decent enough. Golden days! But then Tima got sick. He paid for every week of freedom (my freedom, that is) with two months of constant coughing; he looked so pathetic, all washed out, cheeks almost transparent, he'd just sit around all day getting on my nerves and his own. What do they do to those poor children to make them so mean and aggressive and sick – or is it the children who torture one another? So I stopped taking him to kindergarten and after a while we lost the place; there's a waiting list to get in.

All night I tossed and turned on the divan, the sagging couch in my burrow as Tima calls it, all night I thought and thought and couldn't make up my mind. Dry-eyed and scorched like a fish in a frying pan. Then I looked at the window, suddenly aghast: something white had stuck to the pane! A pale cloudy dawn – the dawn of that ill-starred morning, the morning of my execution, the day of reckoning had arrived at last. If Mother had stayed with us, if I'd put up with this hell, the perpetual shouts and insults, the attempts to 'protect the children from me', and the police and the ambulances . . . as it was we quickly got used to her phantoms – even tried, idiots that we were, to 'expose' her, to argue with her, to demonstrate that the only thing 'standing guard' outside the grocery store was an ordinary cop on duty (as Andrei tried to do, foaming at the mouth, when he came home in a fury from the investigation and Granny, with a crooked smile, nodding out the window at the local bobby informed him 'See, that policeman's standing guard again.' – 'What the hell do the cops care about you?' says Andrei), and I tried to tell her the ambulance wasn't coming for her – it's not coming for you, look, don't

118

you see, they're turning, why should anyone come for you anyway? And then they came for her.

What happened was this: Alyona, day in day out, had been weeping herself hoarse mooching around the apartment, then suddenly started putting on weight and gobbling up all the food, which in turn made Andrei mad with her. Ever since childhood he's kept a sharp lookout to see how much dessert everyone else gets, always charging Alyona – and sometimes even me and Granny – with taking more than our fair share. Everything had to be divided up with the minutest justice; sometimes – he was a real sadist – he'd save half his share for later and set it right in front of little Alyona, just to torment her! He'd really go and do that! Every single member of our family's been a bit twisted as far as food's concerned – it's poverty that does it of course; there were always endless claims and calculations, with Mother openly accusing my husband of 'gobbling up all the children's food' and so on. But I never went in for all that – the only time was when I got beside myself about Sasha who really was a complete sponger and bloodsucker who ate all his children's food, but that was just a result of the shock I'd been through when to my horror I found out the whole story. I'd phoned one of Alyona's friends asking her to have a word with Alyona and tell her she couldn't just weigh into her mother the whole time and never set foot in the institute for weeks on end. Psychiatrists say it really isn't normal, this behaviour – maybe we should have her put in a sanatorium for a while, I suggested

119

on purpose to Veronica, this friend of hers, and Veronica said she didn't think that would help. I'd deliberately chosen Veronica; she was a priggish little so-and-so, member of the Young Communist League – 'sauerkraut' Alyona used to call her – anyway, after a meaningful pause this venomous little Veronica said that in five months' time or so Alyona would no doubt feel much better and would realise in future how to behave herself with boys (if I'd only known then the extent of it – see diary above); as it was there was about to be a public investigation of her personal affairs, though Veronica didn't plan to get involved in any of this dirty business herself – what a good thing, she added, that she hadn't gone to the hayloft with Sasha, whereas Alyona had; there are of course people with pride who don't have to resort to haylofts in the pursuit of happiness, there wasn't a girl that Sasha hadn't propositioned, the whole thing was quite disgusting, she personally had never gone clinging to someone's neck and for her, anyway, masculine beauty resided in something completely different – not in someone's pretty face but in something quite different!

I immediately drew the correct conclusions from all this and over the next month Veronica became my chief ally, while Andrei was coming home from the police and lying down with his face to the wall, and Granny just sat motionless in her little room, stubbornly keeping the curtains drawn the whole time; she'd virtually stopped eating and was terribly weak, once I took her through a bit of something and she squinted at me with her crimson eyes, all the vessels had burst, and then rolled her eyeballs like a

Negress. What she knew or understood it's hard to say, everything took place in silence, all of us were scampering about like mice, Andrei had slipped without a murmur into the jaws of the prosecutor's machine, and I would vanish silently as well, going from the investigator to the lawyer to my meetings with Veronica, and Alyona, all alone in her room, just sat in silence and cried.

But between us in the end Veronica and I managed to put a stop to the personal investigation; she determinedly pleaded Sasha's cause with the dean and ours with Sasha, making sure he did the decent thing by Alyona – at least temporarily, which suited me fine, I needed that fellow like a pain in the backside – see above. In the course of that month Veronica even got quite close to him, chatted away to him, got easy access to the inaccessible secret idol of every girl in the faculty – I gradually came to realise that's what he was, the eternally silent man with eyebrows, I have to admit, like a Turkish beauty's, little dove's wings, and lips permanently parched, Lord help us! Oh the hatred of a mother-in-law, it's pure jealousy and nothing but, my mother herself wanted to be the sole object of her daughter's love – mine, that is – wanted me to love her and her alone, to be the only object of my trust and adoration; she wanted to be my entire family, take the place of everything and everyone else, I've seen female families like that – mother, daughter and small child – fully fledged families, imagine the nightmare! The daughter goes out and earns the living like a husband, supporting everyone else, and the mother sits at home like a wife and scolds the

121

daughter if she doesn't come home on time, doesn't devote enough attention to her child, wastes money and so on, and at the same time the mother's desperately jealous of all her daughter's girlfriends – let alone men, whom she sees as direct rivals – and the result, of course, is always a total mess. But what can you do? My dear mother, before complete disaster set in, succeeded brilliantly in driving my poor husband out of the house and always got her words in on cue: Who's the head of the family, she'd ask (so sly), I ask you now, who's the head of the household round here (meaning, of course, herself).

I moved that Veronica around like a pawn, she was half-crazed with mad hopes on her own behalf, and before us loomed the phantom of this new man who was to enter, sooner or later, our abandoned female household; and it was then – as I say, just as I was beginning to entertain hopes – that Alyona started to swell up and go completely to seed, no longer believing in anything, ready, I realised, to do away with herself once and for all.

And then one day when I came home I discovered that Granny had gone and barricaded her door from the inside, I could barely open it a crack, she'd put the desk up against it. What was she up to, why move the desk, why this blockade? Why put the desk right under the light shade, answer me? I forced open the door and burst into her room, she was sitting all weak and helpless on her divan (the one I have now). Planning to hang yourself, are you? What's all this about?! When they finally arrived with the stretcher she cast one last crazed glance at me, her eyes dilated with tears, tossed her head and then vanished, vanished for good. That evening I went into fearful hysterics, just howled and howled, I couldn't stop myself, Alyona dragged herself in with some tablets and gave me two, I seized the whole bottle from her, I knew very well why she'd been hoarding them and made as if I was grabbing them for myself, I asked her for some water and while she was fetching it I hid the tablets under the pillow inside the pillowcase, still howling all the while. 'Stop these hysterics,' my daughter said to me, and how could I even begin to explain? Tell her I'd been to the hospital where all the windows are barred? That it was the end of our life as we knew it? That Andrei had also been dumped in a hole just like that, behind bars? That I was a criminal? Who'd go and dump their own mother in a psychiatric hospital? I would, mercy on us, that's who! The doctors kept trying to reassure me, telling me we'd be running a terrible risk, that she needed treatment, that it was a long-standing case of schizophrenia, they could tell me the very date it began, she'd told them herself when it was the KGB had started coming after her, I told them the blood vessels had burst in her eyes and they said it sometimes happened. Her eyes were completely crimson. She needs treatment, they told me, her life is in danger.

\* \* \*

So the dull white morning of my execution dawned.

I understood very well that I couldn't take my mother back home, with Tima there I didn't have the right – the last thing he needed was more trouble and fuss, the stench of the menagerie, the shouts and accusations, the urine and excrement, no pension on earth could make up for it all, especially not the mean little one she got. She'd try and make a cup of tea and set the whole house on fire. Lord, I couldn't do it. Tima came in and I smiled at him, as always ('Greet the new day with a smile'), and promised him the bread and butter from yesterday and tea with sweets (Did you have a nice time yesterday?), promised to make him a little house with windows if I could only get hold of some glue. My head ached, I put the kettle on – in my present state, I thought, I'm quite likely to set the house on fire myself, forget to turn off the gas – it could happen any moment, as it was I was amazed this last while that I hadn't once got lost or lost my money or my keys and that I'd managed so deftly to answer my letters, no one could have guessed! No one could have guessed a thing! But if I lose my marbles before I go for good, who's going to save Tima? Who's going to save him? There should always be someone in the house, but where are people to be found, where?

Suddenly there was thunder from the heavens: a ring at the door. Christ appearing before the people. A ring at the door. Who's there? I ask. More of Andrei's so-called friends? I've already paid up, you swine, you dogs, I've given everything I've got! All right, I say. Who's there? I ask, standing behind the door with thumping heart. The kid rushes up to open it – he'd open the door to anyone! Any time!

'It's only me.' Irritably.

'Who's "me"?'

124

'Me, Alyona,' she answers, adding something inaudible.

But this isn't her payday! Has the girl gone crazy?

'What do you want?' I ask in the semi-darkness.

'It's Mummy! It's Mummy!' – Tima's delighted for some reason. 'Mummy, is that you?'

'Yes, it's me,' she answers, weary and irritable, stubbornly addressing the locked door. 'Open up, my darling.'

Her darling indeed!

I unlock the door but leave the chain on, as if to make quite sure.

'What's the problem, Mum?' she asks with fake curiosity. Poor miserable little female. There she is sure enough with her great big eyes. And sure enough there's a new baby in her arms, and there's the second one (yes, the second, the second if you count the whole of her numerous family) clutching on to her skirt. My daughter's decked out in an ancient jacket, miles too small for her and obviously plucked straight from the garbage heap.

'Open the door, open the door,' she tells me. There's a pram, I see, standing next to her – the same old one – and a suitcase and some other bundle. How did she drag them up all those stairs?

'There's no money to feed you here! None!'

I want to slam the door.

The kid starts wrestling with me. On the other side of the door his mother has fished out a key and is fiddling with the lock. But the lock's long since been changed! And the door's on a chain!

Tima pants and struggles. Through the crack in the door Alyona tries to speak to him:

'Don't, Tima, don't even try, she'll crush your fingers in the door!'

'Tima, darling, let's close the door,' I say tenderly.

'No! No!' he yells.

'Tima, darling,' says she, 'don't even try it . . . she's sick! Don't you understand? She'll crush your fingers, sweetheart, she's completely mad! Don't, Tima, move back.'

'That's right, move back!' (That's me.)

'No!!!'

'Move back, darling!'

I gave up. I went to my room and locked the door. I could hear them poking about, then Tima running, and then there was a kind of chirping, another distinct little voice piping 'Goo-joo-doo?' like a parrot. I heard their mother cooing, then they all marched past my door into the kitchen, then into the bathroom. All reunited in a second. A happy family! Tima had saved the day, he'd opened the door, and now he's happy and he's theirs, a member of the family! A mother with her three children. So that's what all the effort was for – that's why I'd spent sleepless nights, gone hungry, nursed him, taught him – just so that Tima in one second flat would come to hate me and chuck me in. Goo-joo-doo. In one second flat my life had lost its meaning. What a clever little creature you are, my darling, what a subtle game you've played. That's right, give everything to your mother, prove your devotion! A little struggle at the door – and there you are! All set! Oh my traitor with your silken curls, your silky little legs! That's how it always ends, the wolf cub runs back to the forest, to Mother! I've seen it time after time: the mother-cuckoo takes over the nest and all her abandoned children flock round and adore her, rejecting in an instant the very person who brought them up! Someone I was friends with briefly years ago – Irina, her name was – I remember her telling me how she'd found out that her supposed mother wasn't her real mother at all, hence their complicated relationship, and now she always went and paid respects to the grave of her real mother, one Astakhova, her adoptive mother having luckily tended the grave all these years – her real mother had died in childbirth, a working woman living in a hostel without husband or family. So this Irina happily went carting her flowers to the grave of this woman while she couldn't give a damn for her true mother, Ksenofontova, the one who'd fed and nourished her with her own blood – Ksenofontova (as Irina had the gratitude to call her – just by her surname, can you imagine!) counted for nothing, no matter that she was seriously ill, had taken to her bed and been forced to leave her job as a Deputy Minister. Meanwhile Irina went and left her husband as well, he was another of Ksenofontova's protégés, the secret son of some bigwig or other among her country neighbours – they all had their government dachas of course – Irina consulted her mother's shade and decided to kick him out, this offspring of the mighty and privileged, and now she lived alone with her daughter, but at least in her own separate apartment. Thinking of this story when I was young I found myself fervently hoping that my mother just like hers would turn out not to be my real mother either and everything would at last fall into place. I didn't feel the least bit sorry for that old cow Ksenofontova, my sympathies too lay entirely at the grave of Astakhova, not with Ksenofontova in her ridiculous man's jacket, her hair cut short with a silly little forelock – I pictured her shaking all over with emotion when she finally made up her mind (feeling she was getting on in years) to reveal to her daughter who she really was and what feats she'd accomplished and what heroic efforts she'd put into it all. Ksenofontova wanted the best and landed up with the worst and her whole life turned out to be for peanuts, for nothing, nothing, nothing at all!

So now it was me who sat there alone, it was my turn to sit with bloodshot eyes on the little couch in my burrow. My daughter was moving in. And there was nothing left for me: no room, no hope. My daughter would take the big room and move Tima's bed into mine. And now she'd be the one to celebrate her solitude in the kitchen at night, just as I'd always done. There was no room for me!

I emerged from my room completely dry-eyed:

'Alyona, can we talk? Are you capable of listening to me?'

She answered as if nothing had happened:

'Just a moment, Mummy.'

Mummy! Break my heart in two!

'You can see we're unpacking. You couldn't feed the older kids, could you?'

'So you've just decided to barge in, have you? Is that it?'

'Tima darling, Katya needs feeding. Can you do it? Grandma doesn't seem to want to.'

'Course I can!' Tima blurts out and takes that fat

128

little Katya by the hand, he walks right past me as if I were a post, leading his sister solicitously to the kitchen. The pair of them tramp by without even noticing me; only Katya pipes up 'Goo-goo?'

'Where are you off to? There's nothing to be had in there!!! Nothing!'

'Grandma darling,' says Tima, 'we've got two pieces of bread and butter and the sweets, I'll put the kettle on.'

'What, must you scald yourself and that child as well!' I shout. 'Alyona, come here, I'm going out.'

'You're going out,' Alyona repeats dully.

Obviously she was planning on going out herself, leaving the whole gang with me.

'I'm going out. Because today' – I announce triumphantly – 'I'm bringing my mother home from hospital. Your granny.'

'Granny?' she repeats tonelessly, gazing at me stupefied. 'Why on earth?'

'Hah! Why indeed! A very good question!'

'Why today? Mum!' she says finally. 'Give it up, won't you! There are three children here!'

'So I see. And in an hour's time if I don't stop them they'll take her to an institution for chronic psychotics. For good.'

'So?' says she.

'So?! Who's going to go and visit her there? Who's going to feed her? Some inmate'll hit her over the head with a stool and that'll be it.'

'You'll go and see her, you'll go and feed her, just as you've always done. Haven't you?' (A caustic hint at something.) 'Or maybe there's something I don't quite understand. What's the great fuss about all of a sudden? You get her pension, don't you? Ah? So what's the problem, you can go and see her.'

'It's about three hours away by train.'

'Never mind. I'm sure you'll want to go and see your mother. Or if you don't you don't. Will you still be getting her pension same as usual?'

'No I will not. When they put them in an institution you know very well they take away the pension.'

'Ah well now, why didn't you say so before, why didn't you explain it was the money you minded about. That's why we're going to have to put up with everyone screaming at the tops of their voices again. That's how we spent our whole childhood, listening to you two screaming. The best years of our lives. There's something completely twisted in our family.'

I reply, dry-eyed:

'That's the very reason I had her put in there, so that you'd have a nice straightforward family, so nothing would be in your way.'

'I've heard these fairy tales a hundred times.'

'To save your family I took her out of your way – for Sasha's peace of mind, so he'd be able at least to tolerate you. But he couldn't stand you anyway!!! No one could!!!'

Her eyes fill with tears – there's something human left in her after all, I notice with an odd kind of satisfaction, she's still capable of shame at her own depravity.

'Mummy, Mummy, don't cry.' Tima suddenly appears at her side.

'Where've you left Katya, darling? You mustn't leave her alone in the kitchen, she'll empty the kettle over herself in a trice.'

'And there's another thing,' I say. 'Our Andrei's being kicked out by his wife.'

'Oh . . . '

'And we know what that means. He's taken to drink.'

(This was not quite the whole truth. When Andrei burst in on me the second time shouting that he was about to be killed, and I was forced to open the door, those same three fellows really were standing there, each with one hand held in his pocket, and Tima was dancing around behind me burning with curiosity. I gathered there was a debt of 800 roubles to pay. I excused myself, shut the door in his companions' faces and said I'd call the police. But Andrei was pale as death and managed to persuade me that they'd kill not just him but Tima too. So the whole lot of us set off to my savings bank and there in front of them I took out everything I had in my savings book, the six hundred and eighty roubles I'd earned with my salt tears and Mother's insurance into the bargain. In return Andrei promised never to bother me again, to get himself a job, stop drinking, have his foot treated in hospital and register his marriage. He was on his knees weeping.)

'What a family!' Alyona gave a lengthy sigh.

'So,' I said. 'Granny will have to go in the small room. I'll move on to the folding bed in the kitchen. If Andrei turns up we'll have to put him in with Granny. He's her grandson after all.'

'He doesn't deserve to be anyone's grandson. I took the children round to his place and he woke us all up careering around dead drunk in the middle of the night.'

'When was this?'

'Last night.'

So that was it.

'He and Nina turned on all the lights and started having a blazing row, that's how he managed to get rid of us. Beat up your own family and strangers will keep away too.'

'He promised me he'd stop drinking!'

'He's been drinking non-stop the entire week, he got hold of some money somewhere and went on a bender with his lovely friends. The place was crawling with them. Okay then, can this room at least be mine – ours?'

'I see, I see . . . well, all right . . . Andrei . . . ' I swallow my tears. 'That's a son for you. That's my son.'

The decision had come completely out of the blue. Freedom, freedom, freedom! How strange to feel free in such a tiny space! And Alyona wasn't going to suffer too much either. What terrible dungeon had she surfaced from if eighteen square metres for four people seemed to her a refuge!

'I'm asking you for political asylum,' she mutters, picking the shoes up off the floor and putting them in a row. She had read my thoughts. 'What a life I've had! Mummy! What a life I've had!'

One moment between us, one moment of truth in the whole of the last three years.

'You shouldn't have had it, you should've just gone and had it scraped out!'

'Scraped out – Kolya? What are you saying!!!'

'Heavens above, girl, everyone has abortions even when they're far gone . . . for money,' I tell her.

'Right up to God knows when. For money!'

'What money? Whose money?' she mutters.

'Theirs! You should have thought about that when you opened your legs to them! And instead you had to take it from us! You slut!' I said from the bottom of my heart, and went off to prepare for the long march.

For the long march. If I don't go now they'll have carried her off. They always take them early, always take them early, they'll have dressed her already in two hospital gowns and gumboots with a towel over her head, it's freezing cold, once they brought her back like that from the X-ray, they'd taken her for the X-ray to a separate building, it meant going outside, when I arrived her bed was empty – Oh what a fright I got, but why did they have to let me see that empty bed? The nurse Marina had let me in, unlocked the door to the ward when I'd tapped with my fingernails, you're not supposed to knock or the patients get worried, they'd warned me then, Rebecca Samoilovna was still working there then, God bless her soul, but now it was hello Marina here's a little something for you, oh no really you shouldn't've, no of course it's for you, dear, it was nothing really, just a little 35-kopeck pen but it was quite hard to find even that, I ran round all the kiosks, all of them were 80 kopecks, the ones with a proper hook, well come in anyway, and she went off with the pen. How the poor kid wept over that – let me draw with that pen, Mummy, he was so taken with it, red and blue and completely new, he won't cry now, he's not mine now, and there's Mother already standing there swaying on her legs.

They'll be putting a dressing-gown on her now and then a second one and a towel, and the hospital orderly will say to the ambulance orderly you'll return the towel and the two gowns to us and the nightie, if you'd sign here please, and my mother's the last in the ward, her neighbour Krasnova's already gone, there's no one left, the ward's gradually been emptied, they've all been sent this place or that, the ward's empty and echoing and Mother lies there following the sound of footsteps with her eyes, they already treat her quite differently, she's the only one left to feed now, she gobbles it all up greedily with her soft toothless maw, soft and bearded and bewhiskered, slack and empty, and her face squeezes up to half its size when her gums start champing and she whispers: 'I'm not going to live,' but you'll live all right, sweetheart, you'll live all right – I mean materially, she says, I won't survive materially – What d'you mean materially, dearie? Now we're going to go off to a nice new hospital full stop. You mustn't go fretting that no one came for you, the state's not going to abandon you is it now, no one gets buried here before their time, you'll always get your bowl of porridge dear don't you worry, and now let's get dressed, shall we, fight the stout fight with all our might, that's the way, darling, they'll look after you there but we've got used to you here haven't we sweetheart, you're the last one out, tomorrow we'll all be going on holiday, whoever heard of going on holiday in February? Just our rotten luck, ain't it, that's right, who's going to need us in our poor old age, oh dear been lying in our poo again have we darling? Better get washed then hadn't we, bring over the bedpan and the sponge dear would you, I'll get the jug and give her a once-over, oh dearie me we have got in a mess now haven't we, just skin and bones is all we are now and to think she had babies once, all starts drooping and falling out don't it? I was cleaning up another old dear, Marina says, and there was this thing just lying there underneath her, it was her womb had come right out, that's what happens you see, you get to eighty-seven and there you are, she's been taken to Hospital Five now, that one, and that's even worse Number Five so I'm told.

There we are now darling, they're going to take you to a lovely new place, lovely and clean, what a one you are though, never stops pooing does she. Aren't ever enough nappies for the likes of you is there darling. Worse than a baby is what you are, now what's all this about. What are you saying? What's she saying? – They should do away with these ones, they really should, stick a needle in them and there you are, what's the point suffering, there we are darling, oh dear oh dear we're all of a tremble aren't we full stop.

But I have to take her something to put on, have to take something now, wait a moment, she's so thin, she'd get into anything of mine, oh dear that's not washed, what are we going to do, that's not clean either, that's torn, what a nuisance, that's when it all comes out in the open, the squalor and poverty! Poverty, yes, poverty, it's the underwear that shows it, just look at these rags, how can we let them see this stuff, well all right, she doesn't need a bra now though they said bring a bra, one set of bloomers . . . bloomers, here's a pair, thank God for them anyway, almost new, kept them at the bottom right at the very bottom just in case for going to the doctor, what a relief now, tears of joy!

Here's a petticoat of sorts, torn as well, what can you do I wear whatever comes to hand, mend and patch things though not all that often, there's no one to see them anyway, what's the point bothering, all come out of the closet now though, oh look at this wonderful exclamation mark a lovely white vest, one of Sasha's leftovers, thanks a lot Sasha, flown the nest now, thanks a lot birdie, bound to come in handy, what's it doing in here though I wonder, ah look now, stockings and suspenders, thank goodness for those, those are the only suspenders I've got mind you, won't fit her anyway, here are some track-suit bottoms though, they'll do, all comes in so handy after all, if I could just find a decent pair of socks, oh dear oh dear no decent ones at all!

All in holes the lot of them I know it, it's the felt boots they always tear stuff, hold on hold on here are some cotton stockings, if I roll them down they can do for socks, now what are we going to do for shoes!

Damn, what can we use for shoes, it's winter, what she needs is felt boots that's what, oh dear oh dear oh dear, where did I put all those felt boots. God what a heap of things we've got in the store room, no way I can sort it all out now, you're a pig, that's what you are, you're a pig, living like a parasite thinking of nothing but that verse of yours, go on, have a good cry then, howl away, I'm never going to make it to the hospital, never going to make it, wah-wahwah!

'God, Mum, what on earth are you doing in there! You're chucking stuff all over the place, I can't get by. Did you really have to go and do this on the very day we came?' (She stalks off.) 'Look what you're doing, for God's sake, kicking up all this dust! Small children about and dust everywhere, ugh!'

I'm never going to make it, never going to make it – hurrah, here are some felt boots and galoshes, hurrah hurrah, thank heavens for that, right, now all we have to find is a dress, a dress of hers, thank God she's smaller than me and I never wore anything of hers or took things apart, once upon a time I'd thought of sewing bits of different ones together and making whole new dresses, but I never got round to it thinking anyway Alyona'll soon be grown-up, soon be time I thought to say here we are darling, I've got all these things laid by for you, you're just the same size as Granny and just the same temperament too, Sharkalina Guzzlegob Hitler, that's what I mentally called her once at one of our farewells when she'd had three helpings of both the soup and the main course, I had no idea at the time that she was pregnant, already quite far gone, and there was absolutely nothing there for her to eat, now then now then, here's a beautiful one!

A beautiful dress, hurrah, Mother's so thin it'll be just right, dark-blue waisted dress, little red and white flower design plus a silk hankie red and white sewn into the breast pocket, Mother was an elegant

young lady in high heels once, those workmates of
hers were a vicious bunch of females, all had fat cats
for sugar daddies, directors and so forth, swine the
lot of them, ah thank our lucky stars here's a decent
coat, nice astrakhan collar, tough blue cloth, you
never see cloth like that nowadays, and here's a hat,
hurrah, oh dear it's all crushed, hard as nails won't
cover the ears, keeping the ears covered's the most
important thing of all, I've told the kid that time and
time again, the kid, the kid, the kid, just don't think
about it, forget it now, no need to cry, no need, he's
there, he's alive, he's with his mother and sister and
little brother, you were just a mat to lie on, he wiped
his soft little feet on you and off he went to his mother, his other mother, she'll cut his hair now, cut off
all his curls and send him to kindergarten five days
a week like the army, I can see it all from beginning
to end – a single mother of three, she'll be top of the
list for the kindergarten, the children's prison, just
hand them over and off to work you go and everything will be just fine

everything will be just fine!

everything!

everything!

but how's he going to sleep there all alone, oh
oh oh, just like your mother sleeps all alone,
shouldn't even think about it, it's been seven years
now full stop, a woollen scarf for her head, the scarf's
with Tima's things, he needs it because of his
earache, it's a checked one, quite decent, ah here we
are, oh it's got yellow spots all over it, must be from
the camphor oil, can't go wearing that in broad
daylight oh dear.

I'm not taking anything I'm not ransacking the place Alyona dear but Granny has to have something to wear on her old head there's not an ounce of fat on it just skull and skin.

and hardly any hair, hardly any!

anywhere!

there's nothing anywhere, there's a thought, I've got that old scarf it's got some wool in it, I wear it round my neck but I don't specially need it it's just for the one time anyway, if I turn up my collar, right, now all we need is a suitcase, a suitcase, where did I put it must be on top of the cupboard, ooof so dusty need to give it a wipe help what's the time the time the time, phew, just need to make the bed up now do we have any oilcloth, Alyona dear, sorry to bother you again, you wouldn't have a spare bit of oilcloth, no I don't suppose so well never mind I'll tear up a plastic bag, or how about I'll ask for an old oilcloth at the hospital they can't refuse if it's written off already, right, run for it

run for it!

run with a heavy suitcase, run the same old way, fifty-two times a year plus New Year plus May Day plus Women's Day plus her birthday, either the ninth or the tenth, I usually go on the ninth just in case, and then the Anniversary of the Revolution as well since dear Rebecca, God rest her soul she was a noble woman, Rebecca just hinted delicately that's when the old ladies feel the worst poor dears on the public holidays they all start weeping and dying off, won't eat a thing and want sleeping tablets, who remembers you now, Rebecca dear, but I do, you were an angel to us, oh God it's so heavy, they've

139

probably taken her by now what am I rushing for it's one o'clock already the ambulance will have come it'll be icy inside she'll be well on her way I'll arrive and oh my God everything'll be locked up the staff on leave the painters inside already, they're the worst-dressed men in the world, I've often noticed, house painters, how many years since I last refurbished this place, oh oh oh oh no point even thinking about it will you let me get by young man I'm about to drop ah thank you good sir I greatly appreciate . . . that's a quote, Oh God look at that crowd at the bus stop the bus is just crawling, how on earth will I get her home if they haven't taken her already that is, is that what you're really hoping you rotten old cow, well we've dragged ourselves here now into the Metro what a din but at least I don't have to change, I hate the Metro such an incredible din, terrible and everyone stares at you, where's she off to that tall woman with a suitcase she looks worried to death and as for her missing teeth, have to remember to keep your mouth shut don't you can't risk a smile, just like the girls at the post office I'd get there and they'd say we were just talking about you, what were you saying, that tall one with the child never seems to come these days? Yes that's it we were just saying that somehow we never get to see her these days that old dear with her grandson, there's a remittance here for you two lots of seven roubles, oh thank you dear that's for my literary work you know, I'm a poet you see, thanks so much you're always helping me out, here dear leave twenty kopecks for yourself, buy some sweets for your little one from me, when my book comes out there'll be a present

140

for you, ouch, ooh, would you mind giving up your seat young lady I can barely stand completely exhausted dropping on my feet, thank you dear, there, off we go!

Go, go, go, still I've put together quite a decent trousseau for her, old people anyway always wear old things, that's what they like, oh dear her brooch, I forgot her brooch, the ivory pin, pin it on the chest helps keep the draught out, well never mind I'll give her my cardigan, oh dear there's a queue for the express won't you let me jump the queue please I'm going to be late, they're closing down the mental hospital, yes, yes, I'm a mental patient you guessed right, yes, certified, come on, comrade, give me another shove will you, oi, give me a hand won't you I can't get on with this suitcase, phew, the express service's a blessing isn't it there used to be just the tram, could you punch my ticket please oh why's that, oh yes you have to pay extra for the suitcase don't you, now what are we waiting for every seat is filled hey coachman get a move on don't spare the horses, off we go now that's the way

run, run, drag the suitcase up the stairs heart going boom boom boom the ambulance must have gone or hasn't it come yet boom boom bang bang bang excuse me for pummelling good afternoon yes I've come for my mother come to take her home I'm not too late am I oh thank God for that thank God for that I'm sorry I should have phoned I was trying to get everything ready, oh dear me I was so worried the ambulance would have gone

oh dear oh dear I'm sorry my daughter just turned up with her three kids poor girl she's all alone everyone's ditched her, everyone, I'm all they've got have to rescue the lot of them, saved my son's life, yes, I'm all on my own a bunch of criminals were threatening to do him in he owed someone some money and I paid the lot he's devoted to me now but he's not well you see, he's disabled, one heel missing, they just tear me to pieces the lot of them, make the porridge rock the baby dress the kid tell the other one a story, of course I'm so lucky, grandmother of three, wonderful grandchildren Tima, Katya, Kolya, lovely names all of them, then there were Mother's things to get ready you can imagine, now what's this you're writing, the discharge certificate, what's that for, diagnosis sluggish schiz. (followed by flourish) yes I see that entitles her to medicine free of charge why don't you just give me the papers you prepared for the institution, just let me have them as a souvenir so to speak, dear – what's your name? Sonya, that's a lovely name too just like sunshine don't hear it much these days straight out of Dostoyevsky, Sonya dear if you'd be so kind

Just a minute, I wanted to give you a signed copy of my verse just as a keepsake, you know, I'm a poet as you know but we had such a to-do today I must have left it at home, well never mind it won't be the last time you'll all be back here again won't you afterwards I'll give everyone a copy

Ah when my book comes out that'll be the day, I'm a poet and poets are God's poor not made for earthly life, they live and die in oblivion, ah yes, now I don't suppose you could possibly, if it weren't for being so poor we wouldn't dream of asking but I don't suppose you could spare us an old bedpan or

142

something a bit of oilcloth perhaps or some old sheets doesn't matter if they're torn I could sew them together but we've got absolutely nothing to put under her, poor Gran, of course you're new here aren't you, my mother here is a veteran you know exclamation mark Oh I'm so grateful to you! Oh, a jug! Oh a bedpan is it and a nice sponge, yes, I understand, and nappies too!! And an oilcloth!!! Never mind, I'll give it a wash! What about some disinfectant, you wouldn't have . . . Never mind, just chuck it all in a heap, the cotton wool too that's lovely, the suitcase'll be empty. Chlorine too, that's marvellous. Now will you bring her here or should I go straight into the ward? Hello dear, hello, how are we? We're going to get dressed now and then we're going home. Shall we do a little wee before we go? I'll put the bedpan under, that's the way, psss psss psss. There we are, let's see. Bravo! She's at least had a pee, she understands perfectly, doesn't she, Sonya, that's marvellous! What about her medicine, Sonya dear, could you . . . I see, you don't give prescriptions . . . But if you'd have a look in her records I suppose they're all written there . . . That's right, Mother, we're going to get dressed. You get up now. Her head's completely bare! They must have shaved her she's completely bald. There we are, well done. Look at your toenails, they could do with cutting, grown out like the devil's haven't they and your fingernails too, who's been looking after you here, never mind, look see here's a lovely pair of bloomers for you and a nice white vest, comes down below your knees but never mind, makes a sort of petticoat, such a tiny little mother we've got, we'll put the boots on later, just hold on to me now we'll put the stockings on top with the long johns underneath and then the boots, the dress comes down to your heels, never mind that's how they used to wear them, ooh my back does ache can't even straighten up, ooh, thank you dear, Sonya's a lovely girl she's brought us a stock of medicines and I'd been afraid to ask, look at her, Sonya, our little doll, goodness, what a smell she gives off, like a sick animal, makes you quite dizzy, you wouldn't have any valerian drops would you Sonya dear, now come on, Mother, get into your boots, is it your nails getting in the way is it –

Stop swaying about, Mother, don't bend your knees, how am I ever going to drag you home, oh Sonya darling thank you so much, glug glug glug, it's marvellous this stuff isn't it, I've never taken anything stronger, oh dear oh dear, Sonya, how am I ever going to get her home, she can't walk at all, you mentioned there'd be an ambulance, I don't suppose you could just tell the driver instead of driving out of town to take us somewhere much closer, such-and-such Metro, it's just seven minutes on foot, I beg you, I haven't got the money for a taxi, I just don't have it, my book hasn't come out yet it will in due course and then I'll be able to pay back everyone I owe, eh Sonya?

'If you're taking her home yourself,' says Sonya severely, 'you can't expect the hospital to do the transportation.'

But just this once as an exception, Sonya dear, if you like I'll go down on bended knee, don't put us through torture, get the driver to take us, there's no doctor here who else can I ask?

'It's up to the driver, ask him.' And off she wanders, not wanting to get involved.

We're all ready and dressed now, Mother sits curled up like an embryo, head bent – a minute longer and she's going to piss herself, I can feel it coming. A clatter up the stairs and an orderly comes down the corridor.

'Patient Golubeva!'

'Over here, over here, I'll be accompanying her, I've got all the documents. Could you just help her manage the stairs, dear.'

Sonya from afar looks on, observes the drama, we descend the staircase, she locks the door from inside with a special key, and that's it, done.

Mother weaves weirdly along in her outsize footwear, bizarre as a puss-in-boots, the orderly, a middle-aged man in white, lifts her by the elbow and under her back, we descend the stairs. Mother's wearing a huge hat, I had to give her mine, she kept bobbing out of the scarf like a cuckoo in a cuckoo clock.

We're in the ambulance.

'Be so kind as to tell me, which way are you going?'

'Number Five.'

'Is that very far? Number Five, I thought they said a different one . . .'

'Far enough. About three hours one way.'

'And after that?'

'After that we come back to town. Not here, to the substation.'

'You know what . . . May I suggest a solution? If you like you can take us all the way to the institution

– it's up to you, of course . . . but if you prefer you can just take us a twenty-minute drive.'

'And where would that be to?'

'I've got all the documents. I can give you the certificate to show I took her home. And that's it. Out of the blue changed her mind, d'you see? And you'll get five hours off.'

'I see, I see. Now listen, lady, what's all this about? If you're taking her home just take her home, nothing to do with us . . . we're not fooling around . . . you just get a taxi and take her home yourself.'

'No no, the thing is, if you won't take her there we'll come with you all the way to Number Five and the head doctor there will give the order for her to be taken back home because she's changed her mind. I'll persuade him to do it, I would have persuaded them here but Miriam wasn't there, you know, the one in charge. I'm telling you that's what they do, you see, they always get an ambulance for these cases, it was just that the head doctor and Miriam were both on leave, otherwise it would have been quite simple. Anyway if that's the case never mind, let's go.'

'Show us the papers.'

'I'll give you all the papers when we get to my doorstep, friends, honestly, don't you see I'm making life simpler for you? She can't walk, you see, she just can't walk.'

'No use trying to get us to transport her, we've got our instructions to take her there, who's going to sign for her otherwise?'

'Well, take her there then, they'll sign for her there, but you'll still end up bringing us all the way

146

back home. I can guarantee. It's not exactly round the corner, you'll be driving six hours in the freezing cold. You'd be much better off telling them at the substation that you took the patient home and that's it, what's the point going all that way?'

'We can make up our own minds what to say thank you very much . . . '

'I can give you the papers for confirmation. And that's it. Think it over now, look at the weather, she might die on the way, God help us . . . now really . . . '

'Okay love, now you get out of here will you! Get out the pair of you! We'll go right back without you.'

'Oh no you won't. You're not going anywhere without us. If you go there you take us with you.'

'Right . . . We've seen a lot of loonies in our time and I can tell you you need putting away yourself! You're an old woman yourself, that's what you are! Old!'

I was shaking all over but the valerian, that precious source of life, did its work as always. Energetic, strong-willed, fully in control, I worked on their thick skulls so powerfully they were ready to slaughter the two of us. They knew very well there was something amiss going on, they were all set to drive off to Number Five, on the other hand they clearly weren't overjoyed at the prospect of driving me around for six whole hours. All the same (I could follow their train of thought) this was a pretty straightforward assignment and if they went back early to the substation they might get sent off God knows where, to fetch a case of the DTs or someone murdered with an axe in a locked-up apartment. That's life.

'I sympathise entirely, I'm sincerely sorry, but there's no way out, I'm accompanying her and I'm going to accompany her wherever she goes, you won't get rid of me. You don't have the right to take her anywhere without papers.'

'What you need is a doctor with a fat syringe!'

An interesting idea: fetch a doctor with a syringe just to get a mental patient home.

'Listen now, in a minute she's going to shit herself right here in your vehicle, she's been fed. I'll take off her clothes, I'm not prepared to wash them all out, and she'll do it right here on the floor (I kept quiet about the bedpan in the suitcase).'

At this point my ancient mother started muttering something, lying there on her berth. I was sitting at the head-end.

They turned round grimly and stared at me.

'Just hurry up and take us home. It's only half an hour from here.'

Cursing, grim as death, the driver turned on the ignition. I shouted out the address. No reaction, didn't budge an inch. Off they drove with us. Where to? It was a complicated route . . . Where on earth were they taking us, where? I couldn't see a thing, they paint over ambulance windows on purpose so as not to worry passers-by. Ah medical secrets, medical secrets, what goes on under cover of them all? Births, rapes, torture, pain, crimes against morality, blood, twisted hands, shouts, cries, the last throes of despair – death. Orderlies are a power unto themselves, despots in their realm who know neither disobedience nor mercy, how dearly this one would have loved to stick a needle in me and show once and for all who was the louse round here and who the boss and tyrant.

Precisely ten minutes later the driver stopped and said we'd arrived. Arrived. How on earth? How did he know how to get to our house – oh, I suppose they must have given him her records, that must be it, but still, but still, it's a difficult place to find your way to, you have to turn in from a completely different side street, those few times – I can count them on the fingers of one hand – when I've taken a taxi . . . where on earth has he taken us, completely the wrong place, the windows are all painted over –

'Tell me, would you be so kind – did you come in the right side? Otherwise you know we'll have rather a walk, it'll be difficult to get Granny there, I realise no one's going to help me, I would have taken a taxi but the pension comes in only the day after tomorrow, you see, that's the problem, can't you tell me where we are, I'm a complete cretin when it comes to geography, ha ha ha! I can never work out how to get anywhere – never know where I am . . .'

'We're there, we're there, this is it.'

I set the suitcase down in the snow and took ages heaving my old mother out, although she weighed nothing she felt wooden, unshiftable. Those two hefty lumps just sat there smoking in their cab and the second I slammed the door the ambulance was off, you couldn't see it for dust. Took to its heels and scarpered like a cockroach.

We were standing somewhere by the side of a road, on a bridge, on a dull grey afternoon with evening drawing on. To our right smoke was rising from a row of tall chimneys, below under the bridge ran railway lines, and for miles around spread an unbroken vista of industrial wasteland. An unfamiliar tram ran slowly past us, muffled by the snow. There were some brick buildings on the far side of the road. A light snow was falling. I was shaking all over. Where were we?

Well . . . but . . . ! It wasn't wartime, we weren't facing the tanks. Those orderlies, of course, had seen straight through us, they knew the whole story inside out. Every day they cart them to and fro, hundreds of bits of leftover human garbage. If they've seen it once they've seen it a thousand times: cunning relatives wanting to take their old folks and children home, refusing this time to yield them up to death and destruction. Seen it a thousand times over, ha ha. One way and another they've had to learn all our tricks.

Encamped on the kerb, unable to move, we were both of us shaking from cold. I set Granny down on the suitcase and she sat scrunched up in her usual pose, like a foetus. Suddenly her whole body shuddered and drooped again, and I realised she had just peed in her boots. Now she was nice and warm. In five minutes she'd be freezing. I hoisted her up by the armpit, grabbed the suitcase and dragged her tiny, scrunched-up, wooden body a bit nearer the tram stop; come what may we'd somehow clamber aboard, someone would help. It would be warm in the tram and we'd be going somewhere.

Behind us a vehicle came grunting through the snow. They'd have to wait. A door slammed.

'Come on then, let's lie her down in here,' said a man's voice. Mother was lifted by the armpits. I turned and followed, dragging the suitcase.

An ambulance was standing by the side of the road. A sudden flurry of snow whipped my face. Someone must have called it, I thought, thank you good people. We went up to the vehicle and a man opened the door. I glanced at him through eyelashes encrusted with frost. It was the very same one, the orderly from the psychiatric transport. They'd come back. Quickly and skilfully he loaded my mother's body into the vehicle and laid her down. I felt the warmth of the ambulance, the light was on. Mother was lying on a stretcher. The orderly covered her wet coat with some rags. Mother lay on the white pillow with her oversized hat like a flowerpot, her sunken mouth and eyes like tiny chinks. Her eyes, her whole face was wet.

'Sign here,' said the orderly and handed me the papers.

So that was why they'd come back. Everything had to be signed.

At home were the children, Alyona, she needed me, and there by the nursery hearth what place was there for this – for the stench of excrement, the urine-sodden clothes, for our old age. Imagine it alongside the sweet smell of soap and phlox and freshly laundered nappies. Why had I scared Alyona with all this, my poor Alyona? It was I who should leave.

The orderly climbed back into the ambulance with my signature, adjusted Mother once more on her stretcher, glancing at me. Perhaps he was waiting for me to say goodbye. Then he climbed out, slammed the door hard, climbed in by the driver, slammed the cab door behind him, and then shuddering the ambulance moved off.

I threw all the stuff in the suitcase on a nearby rubbish tip – the chlorinated nappies, the stinking oilcloth, the bedpan and sponge, my treasures from that brief interval of hope. The torn-up sheets I chucked away too; only the cotton wool I kept.

Now Alyona was really going to land all the children on me, I thought, all three of them, and how on earth was I going to manage, going to and fro to visit Mother. Why hadn't I even wiped her face for her? Why this sudden paralysis – just a routine thing, the orderlies doing God's work, carting an old body off to the almshouse. Why go and sob like that on a bench in the Metro, people kept looking, stupid of me. It's nature, that's all it is, the laws of nature. The old giving way to the young, to the children.

I walked up to my own home, my blessed abode, no need to ring, quietly unlocked the door, it was dark and warm, smelled of babies and warmed-up milk, the empty fridge rumbling in the kitchen, should turn it off really, keep things on the balcony if need be. That's what I thought as I tiptoed into my room, took off all my wet things, had a good wash, quietly steamed myself in the bath and climbed into bed. And now I've awoken in the middle of the night, my time, night time, time to commune with the stars and with God, time to talk and to write it all down, write as I'm doing now.

Total silence in the apartment, the fridge turned off, the only sound the distant thudding blows of Nyura downstairs crushing bones for the children's soup. How many times have I told her not to at night – dull blows that still the heart like the tread of fate. Why such total silence – with three children in the house! Not a squeak from any of them, good children, must be tired. And not a peep from their mother either, good girl, no traipsing around the place to warm the milk or fetch a fresh nappy. All quiet but for those distant blows. The tread of fate. Why are they all so silent?! Good children, sleeping the sleep of the dead. Sleeping like the dead. Total silence. Are they alive, that's the question. Live children don't sleep like that. Without even turning in their beds. It's been silent the whole night. What's the mad girl gone and done to them all – done to herself? Are they alive? Total silence. I've spent my whole life tiptoeing up to the beds of sleeping children, listening to catch the sound of their breath. Sometimes they breathe so quietly it's as if they'd died. Like now. Stop imagining things! Absolute silence! Distant blows. Nyura must be out of her mind, everyone's been complaining about it. She hasn't got enough for the children, buys these bones up cheap. Boils them up for days on end to make meat jellies – well done Nyura, of course, good for her. They're sleeping like the fallen, well done them as well. I can't go in there. Can't find out. Can't begin to imagine it: four coffins in a row, each smaller than the next, and how on earth would I get the whole lot buried?! How on earth, I ask you! Midwinter, the flowers. What flowers can you get in midwinter! Andrei will drink his way through it all. The wretch won't even appear out of terror of me and horror at that poor ruined little life. The wind will ruffle the soft curls on his dead head. They'll look alive in the wind. Loathsome creature, how did she do it? Pills! She's always kept a store of pills. But why the children? The little last one would have needed only a crumb, she must have dissolved it in his milk. The dead wear an expression of relief, like faces after tears. They'll be lying in a row. How long can you go crushing bones, I ask you? Blows of fate. Stop it, Nyura, stop it! Must go and knock on her door. You could go mad. She'll curse me as always, hot-tempered hard-working woman, knows how to shriek the house down. Everyone else has got used to it long since, everyone's asleep. Oh my God! Oh my God!!! Have mercy on us, save us!

I did two things. First, I couldn't stand it any longer and went to tell Nyura. I told her a thing or two in a language she'd understand, told her I'd report her Genka for robbing the telephones if she couldn't understand the simplest things. I'd seen him and so had the children. He'd cut off the receivers. Nyura, standing there in full swing, pounding away, just opened her mouth to let forth a stream of abuse as I slammed her door shut with a bang. Let her think it over. And then. And then I walked decisively back up the stairs, opened the door and went straight into my daughter's room. The light was still on. There was nobody there. A dusty baby's dummy lay crushed on the floor. So she'd taken them all away. A total raid. All three, Tima too. Where had they gone? What did it matter. She'd found somewhere. What mattered was that they were alive. They were alive and all the living had left me. Alyona, Tima, Katya, tiny Kolya, all gone. Alyona, Tima, Katya, Kolya, Andrei, Sima, Anna, forgive me . . . tears . . .